Reviver

BREATHING NEW LIFE
INTO THE DEAD

Christoffer Petersen

Reviver

By Christoffer Petersen

Copyright © Christoffer Petersen, 2023

AARLUUK PRESS

ISBN: 978-87-94119-83-2

www.christoffer-petersen.com

And those who husbanded the Golden Grain,
And those who flung it to the Winds like Rain,
Alike to no such aureate Earth are turn'd
As, buried once, Men want dug up again.

The Rubáiyát of Omar Khayyám

The gladdest moment in human life, me thinks,
is a departure into unknown lands.

Sir Richard Burton

*To Jane
One of the twins!*

Author's Note

Reviver is my B movie. Not in budget, but more specifically in terms of content. The ideas and concepts in *Reviver* are a little wild, and happily unbelievable. I needed to write something different from my usual Greenland crime books and thrillers. I wanted science fiction, but grounded in the familiar. But to be honest, what I really wanted was to write something about dinosaurs!

This is that *something*.

Readers of my other works may struggle to suspend disbelief while reading *Reviver*. Hell, *I* struggled. But I had so much fun during the struggling, that I wanted to struggle some more. So, spoiler alert, there will probably be a sequel. The events of *Reviver* are wrapped up at the end of this book, but as you will see, there is potential for more to come.

Oh, and for those readers who might, just might, have drifted over from the cosy(ish) *Greenland Missing Persons* series, I should add that *Reviver* is full of profanities. Wrangling dinosaurs, apparently, can lead to the occasional swear word.

Or, in this case, lots.

That's it for now. I'll leave you in the capable hands of Luci, Haines, Beane, and Jay, amongst others, and some big old beasts that have returned in the pages of this book.

Chris
February 2023
Denmark

Reviver
Book I

PART
I

1

Warren Elaine Haines, the fifty-three-year-old US Senator for Utah, was late. She was also partially lost. She lost her way somewhere between a cold vanilla latte and a tired cheeseburger, cursing her smartphone and all security applications that blocked *everything*, including Google Maps, which she needed, wanted, and would gladly turn a blind eye to the latest run of memos reminding her why she *shouldn't* use it. According to the god of government memos, she shouldn't even switch on the GPS locator service on her phone. And neither should she call for instructions, directions, or even a fucking Uber. In fact, she guessed what they really wanted was for her to leave the *damned smartphone* at home and use a map.

That's right.

They wanted her to use a map.

She had a perfectly functional GPS mounted to the dash. But no, they wanted her to use a map, the paper kind she might possibly be able to find in a gas station, the kind of map with a hundred adverts printed around the border and a thousand more on the back of it.

Haines pulled over to the side of the road, cursing herself for thinking it was a straight run south on UT 68 to Elberta – which it was – before hanging a right and taking the 36 to Vernon.

Vernon.

When had she ever been to Vernon?

And why was she going there now, late on a Saturday night, blowing off her daughter's gymnastics rehearsal – again – because some guy with a lot of political sway told her she had to be there?

"Okay, maybe it's not *sway*, as such," she said, running her hand through her black shoulder length hair after a moment's pause to check it really was the lights of Elberta in front of her and driving back onto the highway. "But the promise of *sway*."

Memories of a tall, lean man in his early sixties – well dressed with a trim grey beard, body, and the firm handshake to go with it – flickered into her mind as she calmed down and settled into the drive.

"Glenn Adler," she said, as the man's name popped into her mind along with another image of his face – also lean, but with a peculiar scar that bit into his top lip, lefthand side, like an arrowhead. She remembered looking twice, catching the glint of something in his grey eyes, and then swallowing hard to reset, before she let another part of her body drive, instead of the legendary sharp mind and even sharper tongue she cultivated in Washington, D.C. and when necessary, in her home state of Utah. Haines and Adler might have made a good team – her aide had even said so when they compared notes after that first meeting – were it not for Bill Haines and their daughter, fourteen-year-old Tessa, and a marriage that, despite one fling and an affair each, had survived local and national politics for as long as Haines cared to remember.

Headlights flashing in the rear-view mirror distracted her for a moment and she slowed, thinking the car would speed up to pass her, only to discover the driver matched her speed.

"Weird," she said, suddenly acutely aware of the lack of backup or security of any kind. "Not even my damned phone," she said with another glance in the mirror. But Adler had said she would be perfectly safe, and that he wouldn't let anything happen to her. Which was both reassuring and patronising at the same time.

Haines increased speed, slowed through Elberta, then accelerated again on the last thirty-some miles to Vernon.

Vernon.

"Of all the places to arrange a secret meet, Adler had to choose a one horse town with an old backcountry airstrip. Disused," she added, remembering Adler saying something about it belonging to the Bureau of Land Management.

Talking aloud was another one of Senator Haines' trademark traits, but she stopped when the big SUV behind her flashed its lights again.

"What?" She shook her head, as if the driver could see her. "You think I'm going to just stop, jump out and make small talk with a complete stranger in the middle of nowhere?"

The driver flashed again, and Haines slowed.

She glanced at the glove box, imagining the headlines about some crazy senator blasting a kid with her Glock G43X subcompact 9mm – a belated fiftieth birthday present from husband Bill – splashed across every broadsheet, tabloid, and blog from Salt Lake City to *wherever-the-fuck*.

"Nope," she said, slowing again and bumping the wheels onto the side of the road. "I'm not going to be *that* senator." She stopped the car, shifted into neutral, and glanced once more at the glove box. Haines took a long breath. Adler had promised to protect her. This – whatever it was – could be Adler's protection. "I sure hope so," she whispered as she turned her head and watched a black man in his thirties step out of the passenger side of the SUV and jog to her passenger door.

"Senator Haines? Ma'am?"

Haines took a moment to study the man's face – close-shaved, clean – and his smart but practical clothes. She nodded.

"Mr Adler sent me and my partner…" The man gestured at the SUV parked behind Haines' 2015 Ford sedan. He turned back and said, "My name's Jim Beane. Like the whisky?" He smiled, adding, "Kinda."

"Mr Beane?" Haines smiled. "Like that English guy?"

"Well, I wouldn't know about that," Beane said. He shrugged and pointed at the passenger seat. "Any chance I could ride with you? Unless you'd rather I switch with Claud?"

"Claude?"

"No, ma'am. That's *Claudia* Baur. She's

driving the SUV. We're with Rhodium Security, contracted to WARDEV." Beane turned his head as a car approached. Haines saw Beane's slow but deliberate shift of stance, and the discrete but definite movement of his right hand inside his jacket as if he was reaching for a gun. He said nothing more until the car passed and its red lights disappeared from Haines' rear-view mirror. "What do you say, ma'am?"

"Adler sent you?"

"He did."

Haines glanced in her side mirror for a glimpse of Claudia Baur behind the wheel of the SUV, but saw little more than a shadow. She drummed her fingers on the steering wheel for a second and then reached down to press the button to unlock the door.

"Thank you, ma'am," Beane said as he slid onto the passenger seat. He was broader than Haines had first imagined, but otherwise compact; he filled the seat comfortably, but with no excess, which seemed fitting for someone who worked in private – hopefully high-end – security. "If you just keep going," he said, nodding for Haines to drive. "I'll keep quiet. You won't even notice me."

"I doubt that," Haines said. "But…" She pulled into the road and smiled as Baur followed at a comfortable distance. "I could use the company. I was about going out of mind with all this security and the whole sneaky beaky conspiracy theory vibe Adler has going on." She waited for Beane to comment, caught the smile on his lips, and took that as a sign she could continue in the same vein. "You think so too?"

"Adler doesn't pay me to think too much, ma'am. He has other people for that."

"Okay." Haines reached for a bottle of water and tapped Beane's arm with it. "Would you open that for me?" She took it back once he had removed the cap and took a long swallow. "So, tell me, what exactly does Adler pay you for?"

"Mr Adler pays *Rhodium* for the personal protection of all employees, associates, and guests that have anything to do with the project."

"WARDEV?" Haines slipped the bottle into the well of the dash. "I don't even know what that is."

"Mr Adler will tell you just as soon as we arrive."

"And until then?"

Beane grinned and made a zipping motion across his lips.

"Nothing?"

"Not much, anyway."

"Okay…" Haines said nothing for the better part of a minute and then tried a new tack. "How about you? Are you military?"

"I was."

"Let me guess, you were a SEAL?"

"I was a Raider, ma'am."

"And what's that?"

"A Critical Skills Operator with the Marines."

"Oh," Haines said. "You're with MARSOC, then?"

"That's right," Beane said. He grinned, adding, "Special Operations Command. We get up to some stuff."

"Overseas?"

"Mostly." Beane nodded.

"But now?"

"Two kids – twin girls, with one more on the way, and a big floppy-eared dog called Chester." Beane paused as another car approached, and then continued with the cheesy grin that belonged to a tired but content young father. "Michelle thought I should be around a bit more for number three."

"And Chester?"

"Oh, yeah, she's a handful, but Chelle's got her eating out of her hand."

"And the twins?"

A flash of light that had nothing to do with an oncoming vehicle lit Beane's eyes and he smiled. "Yeah…" he said, before falling into a silence that Haines decided not to intrude upon.

I can be nice, she thought, enjoying the fact she was, for once, not sitting with a potential adversary ready to stab her in the political back at the first opportunity. *This is the* nice *me.*

"And take the next left," Beane said, returning from his silent reverie with a lick of professional edge to his voice. "There's a track about a hundred yards after that." He waited for Haines to turn and then added, "It gets a little bumpy."

"A little?" Haines gripped the wheel and slowed as the road surface changed from smooth asphalt to gravel and potholes filled with backcountry shenanigans. "This is Bill's car. He *loves* this car."

"Yeah, well," Beane said, dropping the professional touch for a smidgen of banter. "If you'd chosen a bigger Ford…"

"Beane," Haines said.

"Yes, ma'am?"

"Keep your eyes peeled."

"Ah, yes, ma'am."

"Isn't that what they say?" Haines asked as Beane suppressed a laugh. "Aren't you supposed to be *that guy*?"

"I am *that* guy, ma'am," Beane said. He tapped the dashboard and pointed to a smooth stretch of gravel big enough for two cars. "But as you can see, there's really nothing out here."

Haines stopped the car and turned off the engine. She nodded as the dust settled and Baur parked the SUV behind her. She killed the lights and drew a sudden breath as the darkness descended. The lights of Vernon were far behind them, further north, and little more than a soft white glow on the horizon.

"In Afghanistan," Beane said softly, "the Brits called this kind of space The Great Fuck All, as in there's *fuck all* out there." Beane shrugged and said, "Most of the time they were right, but, you know, there's a beauty in nothingness, and the more *nothing* there is, the more beautiful it gets."

"Beane," Haines said.

He turned, jerking his head a little as if snapping out of another daydream. "Yes?"

"You're not the steely eyed operator I thought you were."

"No, ma'am. I guess not."

Haines pressed her thin lips into a smile and then gestured at the scrub and wide-open land in front of them. "And what now? Do we just wander off into the great fuck all? Or do we wait for a flying saucer to beam us onto the mother ship?"

"Over there," Beane said, pointing. "Do you see that oil can?"

"The rusted red one with the red stripe?"

"The *only* oil can," Beane said.

"I see it, *Mr Bean*," Haines said, giving Beane a taste of her sharp tongue to remind him she was, in fact, a US senator.

"Well, ma'am," he said. "To the right of the oil can is a concealed entrance to a tunnel…"

Haines felt her jaw drop and said, "You're kidding?"

"I guess it's more of a pipe than a tunnel," Beane said, not missing a beat. "But there's a long ladder and a bit of a climb." He pointed at the SUV behind them. "Claud has some extra sneakers that might fit if you need something more comfortable."

"To climb in, you mean?"

"To climb *down*," Beane said.

"And just how far down are we going to climb, *Marine*?"

"Oh, about fifty feet. Deep enough to protect us from the radiation burst."

"What radiation burst?"

"Ah, that's classified, ma'am. But as soon as we get below, Adler will fill you in on everything."

"Adler is underground? Right now?"

"Yes, ma'am," Beane said as he opened the door. "He promised he would keep you safe, didn't he?"

"Yes, but…"

"Well," Beane said, interrupting. "Underground is the safest place. And it's more comfortable than you can imagine."

"Comfortable?"

"That's right." Beane nodded. "It has to be, considering how long we might be down there."

"Wait…" Haines reached for Beane as he stepped out of the car. Her hands clasped a handful of warm air rather than the sleeve of his jacket she was aiming for. She opened her door and joined him at the front of the car. Haines ignored the blonde-haired and pale-skinned Baur as she walked towards them and stopped Beane with her palm pressed to his chest. "You just said *underground, radiation burst,* and something about a *long time.*" She took a breath as he nodded. "Are we under attack? Is this it?" She shook her head as if she couldn't believe what she was about to say. "Tell me, Beane, is this the end of the world as we know it?"

"No, ma'am," Beane said as Haines let her hand fall to her side. "If this was the end of the world, and I knew about it, I would be at home with Chelle, the kids, and the floppy-eared dog." He grinned as Baur whispered the name *Chester.*

"Then what the hell is this?" Haines said.

"This…" Beane gestured at the mountains in the distance. "This is the beginning of the world that once was."

"What?"

"And you, Senator, have been chosen to witness it."

"I don't…"

"This way, ma'am," Baur said with a gentle touch of Haines' elbow. "I have some shoes in your size in the back of the truck." She nodded at the SUV. "If you'll come this way?"

"Yes," Haines said, switching to autopilot. "Yes, of course."

She followed Baur to the rear of the SUV, only to look up at something bright in the night sky – a satellite, tracing a glittery arc in the heavens above them.

2

It wasn't much, but it was home. Lucille Hampton's parents had lived at 52 Badger Street, Churlington Hawley, on the outskirts of Manchester, England, for as long as Luci could remember. She had a vague recollection of a small apartment with damp on the walls – one of her very earliest and briefest memories – but the russet Cheshire brick walls of her parents' house, the bay window out the front, and the old thunderbox with the thankfully disused outside toilet by the fence next to the rail tracks were familiar surroundings, and a safe base from which to start a new adventure. Jocelyn, Luci's identical twin sister, thought so too, and it was agreed that mum and dad would finish what Joshua Hampton dubbed *the last supper* while she picked up her sister from the airport. Luci's dad didn't do *dad jokes*, but he liked to throw a quote or two into conversation whenever he thought he might get a laugh.

"But it's just us, Dad," Luci reminded him on her way out of the door. "You don't have to try so hard. We're your daughters. We're obliged to laugh."

"Best not to get him started on obligations, love," Beth Hampton said, pressing the keys to the Mini into Luci's hands as she pushed her daughter gently out of the house. Elizabeth Hampton had given her daughters her blonde hair, while it was the twins' father who had passed down his long legs and brown eyes. Luci kissed her mum's cheek, clicked the key fob to unlock the car, and waved at her dad as she left the house. She checked her watch as she ducked into the car and cursed as she realised the motorway would be heaving so late in the afternoon and she had better take the back road to the airport. Luci backed out of the drive, bumped the Mini off the half kerb in front of their house, and accelerated along the quiet suburban street.

Jocelyn Hampton's text beeped into Luci's smartphone as she stopped at the single set of lights in the centre of the village of Churlington Hawley. She confirmed she was on her way with a suitably cheeky emoji, and then tucked in behind a tractor heading out of the village. Luci knew the lanes were too tight and had too many bends for her to overtake, and settled into the tractor's slow, if a little maddening pace. She glanced at her hair in the rear-view mirror and wondered what Joci would make of her new look. They had worn the same clothes, shared the same makeup, and even swapped a few of the same boyfriends for much of their early adult life, until Joci made a break for independence when they turned twenty-four with a new look, including a new hairstyle and the kind of piercings that made their dad blush and their mother cry. Joci removed the nose ring six months later but kept the one in her belly button despite repeated infections that suggested it was a lost cause.

"I don't mind the scabs," she told Luci. "But the smell can be a little overwhelming."

Luci didn't like to ask *for whom?* As she wondered how often Joci's nose got anywhere near her belly. But it was one of those sisterly things that was simply accepted, logged, and conveniently forgotten until the perfect moment arrived, usually over dinner when meeting boyfriend number eight, or nine, or the one after that.

The tractor slowed to make the sharp turn into a field and Luci accelerated into the next bend, ignoring the beep of her phone which she guessed meant Joci had landed, and the following two which she knew were probably *through passport control* and *I've got my bags.* The fourth would be an impatient *where are you?* But the lanes were too tight, and Luci's speed was far too fast, to respond.

There was something about driving within one's limits, and then extending those limits – just a tad, that thrilled Luci. She might put words to it one day, adding something in one of her dusty journals about the marked difference between the absolute quiet of a patch of forsaken land, compared to the throaty roar of a small engine. The click and crunch of the gears, and the wash of noise from the mossy stone walls reflected back at the vehicle as she pushed the Hamptons' Mini just a little harder, faster, and more recklessly than her mum would like or her dad would approve. When confronted, Luci would always maintain she had complete control over the vehicle, to which her mum would question if she had complete control over *all* vehicles, suggesting that more than one element of driving was beyond the twenty-six-year-old's seemingly invincible powers. Her dad, on the other hand, would steer the talk in the direction of money – for repairs and insurance. And on it would go until Luci managed to deflect further chiding with mention of Joci's latest piercing or boyfriend number eleven or twelve.

Luci slowed as she reached the main road, slipped into traffic, and then took the series of roundabouts to Terminal 3 of Manchester Airport, cursing the new fares system that had the taxi drivers up in arms, and car park companies rubbing their greedy little hands. But Luci forgot all about the trials of parking when she spotted Joci standing on tiptoe for a last goodbye kiss with boyfriend number thirteen. Luci gave her sister a blast of the horn and another when Joci flipped her the finger.

"Honestly," Luci said, waving at the twenty-something man Joci left outside the airport as she got out of the car to greet her sister. "What are you wearing? Fly paper?"

"I'm going to ignore that," Joci said. She collected her shoulder-length blonde hair into a short ponytail and secured it with a rubber band from her wrist. Then, taking a step back, she tilted her head to one side to give her younger sister the once over. There were just six minutes between them, and Joci used every last one of them. "Have you put on weight?"

"Muscle," Luci said. She took a step closer to Joci, anticipating the long-overdue hug, but keeping her hands at her sides as she respected the ritual that preceded it.

"And your hair?"

"New," Luci said. "And you like it."

"I do."

"Jealous?"

"*Not*," Joci said with a shake of her head.

The bustle of passengers, the burr of small plastic suitcase wheels across the tarmac, and the constant opening and shutting of car doors and boots filled the air around the two sisters, but caught within their own intimate bubble, they ignored it.

"It's been too long," Luci said, reaching for her sister.

"It's only been five months," Joci said, but returned Luci's hug with such enthusiasm that passers-by might think the twins had been apart for at least a year, possibly longer.

Luci was the first to let go, brushing her older sister's cheek with her lips, before reaching for the backpack Joci carried casually over one shoulder. "It's a shame we've only got the one night."

"I know," Joci said. "Let's make it a night to remember." Her eyes twinkled in the afternoon light as she smiled and Luci sighed as she guessed Joci had plans for their leaving ritual, just as soon as their parents had gone to bed. She let Luci take her pack and then pointed at the car. "You took the back roads?"

"Had to," Luci said as she stuffed Joci's pack into the tiny luggage space at the rear of the Mini.

"It's covered in shit, Joci."

"Yep."

"Dad's gonna love you."

"He does," Luci said with a nod to the passenger seat. "Enough to put me on the insurance and not you."

"That ticket was not my fault." Joci waggled a finger at her sister as they grinned at each other across the roof of the compact British classic. "I just happened to be on the wrong road at the wrong time."

"It wasn't the wrong *road*," Luci said. "You just picked the wrong *policeman*. Not *all* men are susceptible to the charms and wiles of Jocelyn Hampton, sis." Luci laughed as she opened the driver's door.

Joci shrugged and nodded at the man still waiting for his ride outside the airport. "That one was," she said.

Luci sighed and said, "You want to give him a ride?"

"God, no." Joci wrinkled her nose. Followed by, "Just *no*." She opened the passenger door and said, "Just take me home before you make me change my mind."

Luci waved one last time at the man, giggling as Joci dug her fingers into the waistband of Luci's jeans and pulled her into the car.

"Luci!"

"All right. All right," Luci said as she closed

her door. "We're leaving."

Joci tightened her seatbelt and then tipped her head back as Luci backed out of the parking space. She closed her eyes, singing along to *Have A Nice Day* by Stereophonics as Luci slipped their favourite CD into the compact modern unit jury-rigged to the Mini's ancient cassette player.

"Home soon," Luci said, as she slipped the Mini into the airport traffic.

Home on Badger Street was the only *home* Joci said she could remember, and even though it had only been five months, she took the usual tour of the house once she had escaped her mum's hug and dad's goofy antics as he searched for the boyfriend he was sure the girls had left in the car.

"Don't look at the car, Dad," Joci said, flashing Luci a cheeky grin as she successfully deflected Joshua Hampton's attention to her younger sister, and the speed which with she must have been driving to make such a mess of the Mini.

Luci resigned herself to the lecture she knew was about to erupt from her dad, while wondering if it was even worth reminding him – *again* – that she had just turned twenty-six and that she wasn't *daddy's little girl* anymore.

Neither of them were.

But neither did he nor their mother know the true destinations to which their daughters were headed the following day, and she endured his parental rant, taking his hand when his blood pressure got the better of him, just as she knew

Joci would do when he revisited the question of relationships somewhere between the end of dinner and the nightcap he felt he deserved before heading up the stairs to bed.

Dinner passed and the lies, like the red wine, flowed to and fro across the table as Luci told them all about the archaeological dig she had been invited to visit in the Mojave Desert, California, while Joci gave an equally enthusiastic account of her upcoming internship with the latest hot NGO at their headquarters in Belgium. It wasn't until *the girls* tidied up in the kitchen that they whispered their true destinations while mum and dad put their feet up in the lounge in front of *Strictly Come Dancing*.

"Libya," Luci whispered. She nodded as Joci raised her eyebrows. "A little east of Harat Zuwayyah."

"Okay." Joci dipped her head around the open doorway separating the kitchen from the lounge area. "That's full on," she said. "It's still a dig, though?"

"Of course," Luci said. "Records of dinosaur fossils and finds across Africa are patchy at best. We're hoping to do something about that."

"You and…" Joci paused as if she was searching for a name, only to smile as she pretended to remember something she had never forgotten. "Sugar Albuquerque," she said. "I *love* that name."

"You'd love her, too, if you ever met her." Luci reached for Joci's arm and gently grasped her wrist. "You could come with me. Then you'd meet Sugar and…"

"Nope," Joci said. "No can do."

"But you said you were going to Africa?"

"Further south," Joci said. "To Gazania."

"Where's that?"

Joci shrugged and said, "No one knows. And that's the whole point."

Luci let go of her sister and leaned against the kitchen counter. "You always were the adventurous one."

"Says you?"

Joci spun the tea towel into a loose coil and snapped it at her sister. Luci cupped her hand into the dishwater and responded with a handful of bubbles aimed at Joci's head.

"That's it," Joci said, as she reached for a second tea towel.

Luci grabbed an empty cup, filled it, and prepared to defend herself.

"Everything all right, girls?" Beth Hampton called from the living room.

"Everything's fine, Mum," Joci said. "Just dealing with some stuff." She pointed at the cup of dishwater in Luci's hand. "Don't even think it," she hissed.

"Wouldn't dream of it," Luci said, even though they both knew she would, that she had – many times – and at the risk of spoiling *Strictly*, she was ready to do it again. "I won't if you don't," she said.

Joci bit her bottom lip as if she was thinking about it. And then, tossing the tea towels onto the counter, she pulled a small bottle of Jack Daniels from the cargo pocket of her trousers.

"Let's get them to bed, then we can talk," she said, slipping the bottle back into her pocket. "I want to know everything. All right?"

"Deal," Luci said. She glanced at the doorway and when the judges were giving feedback to the dancers, she flung the dishwater into her sister's face.

"*Girls!*"

Luci barely heard her dad shout as Joci's shriek filled the kitchen.

"Look at you," Joshua said as he stepped into the kitchen. "When are you going to act your age?"

"Tomorrow? Maybe," Luci said as she smiled at her dad, just seconds before Joci lunged for the plastic bowl of dishwater.

3

The light from the street twisted shadows onto the walls of Dr Chandler Green's New York apartment. He could have drawn the curtains, dropped the blinds, or even just closed his eyes, but there was a random beauty in the shadows, and he spent another hour sipping a tall glass of bourbon, imagining the people throwing shapes on his walls. The possibilities were endless, as infinitely unique as the people of New York themselves. Green raised his glass at the latest shape – an elephant with an umbrella – and toasted diversity, followed by another toast to independent thought, free will, and all the other crap he subscribed to when he wasn't drunk, depressed, or *dead to the world* as one colleague put it.

"You have to publish," his colleague had said. "*Anything.*"

But Benjamin Shoot, PhD., didn't understand NDA's like Green did, and he sincerely hoped he never would.

A Non-Disclosure Agreement was standard fare in Green's field of Applied Distant and Far Future Stellar Radiation, and the concepts so obtuse no one, save a few men and three women in the field, would know what he was writing about, anyway. But whereas the money was good, the organisations with the purse strings to even contemplate dipping their toes into Green's field, were either governments – the rich kind – or billionaires with an itch to be remembered for advancing one field or another, the more profitable the better.

There was profit in the stars. Everyone knew it. But grasping concepts that could be understood, applied, and developed beyond a fancy three-dimensional simulation was not, Green knew, the best return of investment for anyone or any *body* with the means to invest.

Glenn Adler, taller, trimmer, and with more hair than Green, despite being twenty years the scientist's senior, was the first to reject the impracticalities of ADFFSR or Future Applications of Stellar Radiation which he then dubbed FASR which was a much easier word to morph one's lips around. FASR became *phaser*. And, before he could stop himself, Green agreed to set his *phaser to stun*, and present the wildest application of the as yet undefined, unexplored, and wholly unproven unimaginable stellar radiation he could dream of.

Green called it *Ceti Radiation*, with a nod to the distant sun *Tau Ceti*, and the promise *that* system held for future wonders and possibly even neighbours.

"If we ever reach it," Green said, raising his glass to what appeared to be the shadow of a squirrel riding a bicycle. He turned his glass in the light, swirled the liquid inside, and grinned at the last grains of his favourite opiates he had crushed before sliding the powder into the glass and spilling a generous…

"Be honest, Green."

…spilling a hefty and *adventurous* measure of bourbon on top of it.

The crazy shadow play continued as Green sank deeper and deeper into his mind.

While he would never admit it, Green did his best work when he was suitably *juiced*, as he called it. The *juice* part came at breakfast when he splashed fresh orange juice, more drugs, and even more bourbon into the same glass, while purring new ideas, thoughts, and areas for analysis into the microphone. He jacked his laptop into the seventy inch flatscreen television mounted on the wall of his sparsely furnished but comfortable lounge, and watched as the words materialised on the screen. Green stopped to stare at the words as he drifted from the dead dark of deep night, into the skull-splintering pale dawn before the bright light of a new day sent him cowering beneath the blankets he dragged from his bed onto the futon he had in the lounge.

He stared at the words, nodding in the knowledge that there was gold in the jumble of letters, typos, spins of syntax, and scientific apologies he slurred onto the screen.

Green made a point of never editing the *juicy bits*, as he called his late night-early morning sessions, but would trawl through them once he was sober and had slept off the effects of his drugs of choice. If Adler knew what it took for

Green to *work*, he never mentioned it.

"And why the fuck would he?" Green said, fiddling with the microphone clipped to his collar as he conversed with the spectral form of the thinnest baboon he had ever seen as it gambolled from one wall to the next. "He knows it's gold… Fucking gold," he said, to which the baboon simply disappeared. "Fine," Green said, waving his glass. "Fuck off, then. Don't listen to me, you might learn something."

And then he collapsed – more of a slow, predictable topple, like the felling of a rotten tree made of molasses. Green sank to the pinewood floor, priding himself with the last slow blink of an unfocused eye as he managed to set his glass down on the floor before hitting his head and drooling onto his collar.

"Green," Adler had said when they met a year earlier. "You look like shit."

"It's my default look," Green had said. Adler slid a cosmically dark cup of coffee across the table to Green and waited for him to take a sip. "Thanks," Green said.

"Feeling better?"

"Feeling…" Green said, leaving it at that.

He leaned to one side, blinking in the light from the street that poured through the panoramic window, lighting the aisle running between the booths and the first line of tables between Green and the counter. He rolled back again, gripping the table for support, before settling against the high-backed booth and taking another sip of coffee.

"Finish it," Adler said with a nod at the mug. "I'll leave you to… *Whatever.*" He made a vague gesture with his hand as he slid out of the booth, adding, "I'll order breakfast."

"No fats," Green called out after him. He turned to the couple sitting closest to them, apologising for raising his voice. "I'm fat intolerant this morning," he said, by way of an explanation. The couple smiled and Green returned to his coffee, searching for Tau Ceti in the coffee's depths.

Adler found him slumped over the table ten minutes later.

"You're a mess," he said, pushing Green into an upright position before he sat down. "How often do you do this?"

"As often as I need to," Green said. He blinked as the waitress returned with two plates of hash browns, eggs, and sausage. "I said no fats."

"And I didn't listen." Adler smiled at the woman as she set the plates on the table. He waited for her to walk away before continuing. "How many sessions did it take to stumble onto the ceti particles?" Adler reached for his knife and fork, nodded for Green to do the same, and then started to eat.

"The first session was biblical," Green said. He sighed before forking a bite-sized length of sausage into his mouth. He chewed, swallowed, then turned to the couple opposite. Green raised his voice a little and said, "Today I do fats."

"Today," Adler said under his breath, "I'm

earning my money."

"Ah, money," Green said, feigning a sudden alertness he neither felt nor projected. "How much more are you willing to give me?"

"Like I told you," Adler said. "As much as necessary, and more than you'll ever need."

Green pointed his fork at Adler and nodded. "That's why I like working with you."

Adler shook his head. "No, you don't, Green. You just tell yourself that in that dark hour just before the dawn."

"Dylan," Green said with another nod. "I don't listen to enough Dylan."

They ate in silence for several minutes. Green nodded at the couple when they left the table, and then again when the waitress returned to top up his mug of what he had decided was his new favourite coffee.

"Colombian," she said, when he asked. "Night Shade, or something." She left with a shrug, bringing filling mugs with cosmic measures of Colombian coffee at each table she passed.

"Okay, Green," Adler said, sliding their plates to one side. "What have you got for me?" He reached for Green's notes as he took them out of his satchel and spread them on the table between them.

"You won't understand them," Green said. "*I* barely understand them."

"Walk me through them anyway," Adler said. He leaned back as Green reordered his notes, pausing as Green hesitated, before reaching for his coffee as Green talked him through it.

"We've talked about ceti particles piggy-backing gamma waves. Remember?"

"I do," Adler said. "Gamma waves are pure energy. They'll go through anything but the thickest lead or concrete."

"Right," Green said. "Then we've got the particles. Alpha are the biggest and heaviest. But they're so big and so heavy, they can't travel very far from the source."

"Decaying material," Adler said.

"Right again. It's why we get zones of contamination. Meaning, we can put a ring around them. But beta particles are lighter. They travel further. They're small, fast, and have better penetration. But they have less impact on DNA because the ionisations are more widely spaced." Green shuffled the papers until a particularly crumpled sheet riddled with notes and arrows was on top. "Ceti particles are stellar," he said. "Stellar in every way."

"You've told me this."

"I told you they existed," Green said, holding up a finger to prevent further interruption. "But I never told you why you should be interested in them." He reached for his coffee, took a sip, cast an admiring glance at the cosmic liquid as if he could see the stars in the depths of the night sky within it, and then, encouraged by an exaggerated clearing of Adler's throat, he continued. "I said ceti particles piggy-back on gamma."

"You did."

"And that's what makes them special. You

said it yourself; gamma waves are pure energy. They have no mass. They take some stopping." Green turned the paper to show a crude drawing on the reverse side. "Ceti particles originate in space. Just like alpha and beta particles, they come from decayed and decaying material. But..." Green bobbed his head as if searching for a simple explanation. He glanced at his plate and saw the grease congealing on one side and nodded. "Ceti particles are greasy. Gamma waves pass through most of them, but if the gamma rays pass through a dense cloud of ceti particles. And I mean, *really* dense," Green said.

"Then some of the particles stick?" Adler frowned. "I didn't think that was possible?"

"It wouldn't be if it weren't for the cosmic charge."

Adler's frown deepened. "And now you've lost me."

"Yeah, I can see that." Green held up his fists. "Alpha particles are positive. Beta are negative. They should react..."

"Like a magnet?"

"Sure," Green said. "But gamma radiation is photons, not particles. There's nothing to react to. So..." Green opened his fist and slid his palm through the air above the table. "It just cruises with nothing slowing it down and nothing stopping it."

"Until the ceti particles catch a ride?"

"More like catching a wave, like surfing," Green said. "Only the greasiest particles – the cosmically charged ones – will stay on that wave.

But they're the ones we're interested in. They're the heaviest."

"And penetration?" Adler said, lowering his voice. "The ceti particles are riding the gamma wave. Do they ride the wave *through* things?"

"I think they do."

"You think?"

Green gestured at the papers and said, "None of this is proven. We haven't got any ceti particles to play with. Basically…" He shrugged and said, "I made this shit up."

"But you believe in it?" Adler said.

Green caught the look Adler gave him, the tone in his voice, and, regardless of the massive amounts of money he could expect to be deposited in his bank account, Adler's willingness to support Green's *shit*, as he described it, was unnerving, bordering on terrifying.

Adler broke the tension with a soft laugh.

"You just had a Manhattan Project moment, didn't you?"

Green swallowed. "I think I did."

Adler waved his hand for Green to continue. "Ceti particles," he said. "Riding gamma waves."

"Yes," Green said. "Even if some of them don't penetrate…"

"The greasiest ones will go through?"

"All the way," Green said. "And they'll do some serious shit when they do."

"And what kind of *serious shit* would that be?" Adler asked.

"I don't know," Green said with a shake of his head.

"Care to speculate?" Adler took out his Cryptophone, entered a sum of money on the screen and turned it towards Green. "How about now?"

Green took a breath and then reached for his coffee.

"This really is good," he said. Adler waved for the waitress to bring more. She filled their mugs and Green girded himself with another sip. "It's just a theory," he said when the waitress was gone.

"Theories are what I pay you for," Adler said. "Go on."

"Well," Green said. "Without knowing I'd say there's a good chance the combination of ceti particles riding gamma waves presents us with…"

Green put his coffee down and drummed his fingers on the table.

"Green…" Adler said, waiting.

"Okay. Fine. Fuck it," Green said. He leaned forward to prod the paper with his finger. "I think ceti particles could be big bang stuff, only on a tiny scale."

Adler's frown returned, and he said, "And what does that mean, exactly?"

"The big bang is how we came to be," Green said.

"Yes?"

"Well, on a smaller scale, but concentrated on an area, like a dead cell, for example…" Green paused for a beat and then said, "I think it could bring that cell back to life."

"You're talking about rejuvenation?"

"No, I'm not," Green said. "Rejuvenation suggestions restoring something, as if it was dormant…"

"Like a dormant cell?"

"Yes," Green said. "But I'm talking about *dead* cells. I think a concentrated blast – maybe even a tiny blast – of ceti particles could *revive* a dead cell, maybe even a bunch of dead cells, and bring that cell…"

"Or that *thing*," Adler said.

"Sure. That *thing*…" Green nodded. "I think ceti particles could bring it back to life."

Adler took a moment, nodding as he looked at Green. He made a note on his phone, and then leaned forward, gesturing for Green to do the same, until their heads were nearly touching.

"These particles," he said.

"Yes?"

"If they can do this, why haven't they already done it?"

"There's nothing to say they haven't," Green said. "Just not in our neck of the woods."

"So all this…" Adler gestured at Green's notes as he leaned back in his seat. "All this is based on something you think might exist, but have no feasible idea how we can even get hold of it if it does? Does that about sum it up?"

"Yes," Green said. "There's no point lying about it. I told you I made this shit up."

"You did," Adler said. He spread Green's notes on the table and took a photo of both sides of each piece of paper. He shuffled them into Green's hands when he was finished. "Not a word," he said as he slid out of the booth.

"Does it even matter?" Green said. "Even if I'm right, there's no way we can get hold of this stuff." He waited for Adler to respond, adding "Is there?" when he didn't.

"Keep working," Adler said. "I'll be in touch."

"Hey," Green called out as Adler turned to leave. "You never answered my question."

Adler turned and looked Green in the eye. "Because I don't have to, do I?" he said.

Green slumped in the booth as Adler walked away. He reached for the coffee, drained it, and then reached for Adler's.

"I'm going to need something stronger," he said as he watched Adler call for a cab outside the diner. "A lot stronger."

4

Saturday nights at the *Bull and Bush*, within spitting distance of Fenway Park in Boston, Massachusetts, had a certain charm, something Gunnery Sergeant Jay *Warbird* Styles appreciated from the first English dark ale to the last. Eighties night took the experience to a whole new level as the synthesizers synced with Jay's memory of the tunes his mother used to play, the way she would take his small hands and dance around the tiny living area of their one-bedroom apartment, how his stomping would make the neighbours thump the ceiling below and the walls to both sides. Jay's mom was usually too high to care, and four-year-old Jay was too young to know any different. Twenty-eight years and five combat deployments later, Jay enjoyed the fact he could still remember something from so long ago – his mother, her pale white skin, red hair, and bright-eyed smile – when more recent memories were more elusive, such as the question of whether or not he had paid his tab, and just how many pints he had consumed between the first and the last. Jay thought it was five. Frank, behind the bar, said it was seven. Bob, the manager, said it was enough. And Tim… Was his name really Tim? *Tim*, the bouncer, said nothing at all. Which was a mistake, as Jay tried to explain when Tim grabbed a fistful of the back of Jay's heavy cotton shirt as he tried to drag him to the door. If they'd talked, exchanged but a few simple words, then Tim might have known what old Warbird's platoon knew all too well, that the difference between six and eight was elementary, as it was only after eight pints that Jay Styles lost the power of speech and movement. Anywhere between pints one and seven, he was lethal. The marine corps made sure of it.

"You need to let go of me, man," Jay said, slurring his words as he found his feet.

Tim said nothing.

Bob opened the door.

Frank picked up the phone, dialling just as Jay shrugged out of Tim's grip and spun to face him.

Tim, or *Timothy* as his mother called him, was a big fella with a temporary worker visa, giving him enough time to find a nice American girl to fool around and fall in love with to make his time in the States more permanent. His British accent made up for a rather flat face as he charmed the girls with his quaint English curses and curiously cute lisp. Tall for a Brit, his height and build, combined with his accent, made him the perfect doorman for the English pub, as he slipped into the local ex-pat scene, making friends, and opening doors among the regulars who called the *Bull and Bush* home.

It's good to have friends.

Especially in times of need.

And when Jay squared his feet on the tacky

wooden floors of the English pub, Tim needed all the friends he could get.

"I told you to let go," Jay said as Tim leaned in to grab him once more. Jay slapped the bouncer's hand away, took what he thought was a firm step backwards, and bumped the elbow of another large Brit enjoying his second pint of the evening. "Sorry, *mate*," Jay said, offering the man his cheesiest smile to accompany what he considered his best British accent.

"You fucking yank," the man said as he slopped beer into his lap.

Jay took another step backward, then pivoted – slower than he intended, but still *fast enough* – as Tim moved in a second time. The scrape of the chair on the floor as the man with the beer-sodden crotch stood up was the trigger snapping through Jay's beer-fuddled brain as he made a new threat assessment. While Jay's reaction was slower than his platoon might remember, it was still faster than Tim or the slighted drinker could anticipate. Jay removed the immediate threat with a single fist to the drinker's sternum, and followed up with a swift kick to Tim's right shin, dropping the bouncer to one knee at the same time as the first man hit the deck.

"Frank?" Bob yelled as four of the regulars put their pints down to join the fray.

"He's on his way," Frank said, with a wave of the phone. "Five minutes."

"Five?" Bob cursed. "This'll be over in three."

Two minutes and thirteen seconds, according

to the videos the police collected from the pub patrons once they arrived twelve minutes after Jay had cleared the room. The gunnery sergeant wobbled and swayed in the eye of the storm when Malcolm Connor entered the pub. Jay blinked through a stream of blood as he raised his fists to meet the new threat, curious that there was something familiar about the short white man in the hoodie.

"Stand down, Gunnery Sergeant," Malcolm said as he took a cautious step closer. "You're done here."

"I'm done?"

"Tangos down." Malcolm gestured at the bodies crumpled and groaning on the floor in a ring around Jay. "Time to get you home."

"Home?" Bob pushed his way through the ring of patrons filming the fight. "Not *home*." He stabbed a crooked finger at Jay. "He's going to jail."

"Not tonight," Malcolm said. He nodded at Frank behind the bar. "Agreed?"

"Let him go, Bob," Frank said. "We'll sort it out later in the week."

Malcolm took another step closer to Jay, then slowly raised his hand, waving it in front of Jay's face to catch his attention. "Let's get you home, Warbird," he said, as Jay lowered his fists.

Home was a one-room apartment not much bigger than the one Jay spent the first few years of his childhood in. Malcolm waited as Jay fumbled the key out of the pocket of his jeans, and then again as Jay struggled to put the key in the lock.

"I got this," he said as he prised the key from Jay's grip and opened the door.

"Thanks." Jay stumbled into his apartment and slumped onto the sofa as Malcolm made coffee in the kitchenette on the other side of the room.

"The war's over, Jay," he said, pressing a mug of black coffee into Jay's hand.

"Well, that one is," Jay said, sobering up fast with gulps of strong coffee and the breeze from the window Malcolm opened to air the room. "How much is it going to cost me?"

"A bit," Malcolm said. "Although I think it's going to cost me more." He shrugged when Jay frowned at him. "Frank's an old friend of the family. That's the second time I've dragged your sorry ass out of that pub." Malcolm gave his friend a quizzical look and said, "Just when was it you decided to wage war on the English?"

"Tuesday," Jay said.

"Right." Malcolm laughed and then sat down on the threadbare chair opposite Jay. "Tuesday."

"It could have been Monday." Jay took another gulp of coffee and then set the mug on the low table between them. "It's all been a bit of a blur since I got back."

"About that," Malcolm said. He waited for Jay to look up before continuing. "Rhodium has concerns."

"*Rhodium* does? Or you do?"

"Both," Malcolm said after a pause. "This self-destructive path you're on doesn't mesh well with the company. Contrary to popular opinion and what the good folks at CNN have to say about private military contractors, Rhodium has a solid reputation." Malcolm paused again. "Untarnished," he said. "You feel me?"

"Yeah," Jay nodded. "I feel you."

"This…" Malcolm gestured at Jay, pausing as he focused on the week-old bruises on his cheeks and the blood tricking into the chin strap beard on Jay's square face. "It's not a good look for the company, and it's not a good fit for the team."

"*My* team?" Jay leaned forward, suddenly alert. "You're saying my team has a problem with me?"

"I'm saying…" Malcolm lowered his voice. "I'm *saying* there are concerns, and your future at Rhodium has been discussed."

"By whom?"

"Head office," Malcolm said. "They're concerned about the *spiral of violence spinning out of control*. End of quote." Malcolm grinned, then laughed as Jay shook his head. "I thought you'd like that one."

"I'm spinning out of control?"

"Well, you were *spiralling* more than a little in the bar, that's for sure."

"Yeah, okay," Jay said. He slumped on the sofa, ran his hand through his thick black hair, and then picked at a scab of newly dried blood.

"But," Malcolm said, "there is a solution."

"No." Jay shook his head.

"You don't know what I'm going to say."

"Yeah, I do." Jay pushed himself off the sofa

and grabbed his mug. "I'm not going to Libya," he said as he poured another mug of coffee. He opened the refrigerator and grabbed a cardboard box of leftover noodles, then searched the drawers for a clean fork.

"It's a cushy number, Jay. Setting up a security zone in the middle of an empty desert."

"In *Libya*," Jay said as he found a fork cleaner than the rest and carried his noodles and coffee back to the sofa. "It's a punishment detail. You're sending me to the desert to get rid of me."

"It's not *all* desert," Malcolm said. He shook his head when Jay offered him some noodles. "There's an oasis. A watering hole."

"Yeah, in the middle of the fucking desert."

"It's that or..." Malcolm shrugged. "Actually, it's only that."

"Or I'm out?"

"Out with a reputation that, honestly, limits your options to cowboy outfits like *Valkyrie* or..."

"Don't say it," Jay said with a mouthful of cold noodles.

Malcolm grinned and said, "*Limestone*."

"*Brimstone*." Jay sighed. "If you're going to fucking say the name..." He left the sentence unfinished and returned to his noodles with a shake of his head.

"Right," Malcolm said. "But *Brimstone* are the only guys who will even look at your resume – regardless of your deployment history." Malcolm leaned forward and said, "Just consider it."

"Libya?"

"Yes, *Libya*. It's not as bad as you think."

"No one wants it, Mal. You're offering it to me like it's some kind of redemption. But really, you're offering it to me because you've got no one else. Rhodium was too quick and too greedy to say no. And now it's your headache. Am I wrong?"

"You're not wrong," Malcolm said. "But you don't have all the facts. This is a government gig. Sure, you wouldn't know it. It's been served up as something from the private sector, but it has US government fingerprints all over it. And not the usual crap. They've chucked some money at this, Jay. The gear is top of the line. Better than what you're used to." Malcolm nodded as Jay stopped eating. "That's right," he said. "Better gear, better pay. Your team has already said yes. They're just waiting for you."

"Jazzman and Sparrow said *yes*?"

"They did. Even Marion is onboard, and she's bringing Scruffette."

"She's taking her dog to Libya?"

"She is."

"Huh," Jay said. He slid the empty noodle box onto the table and reached for his coffee. "She said, after Afghanistan, she'd never take her dog to another desert again."

"That's what I'm saying." Malcolm laughed. "And I can see," he said, pointing at a spot between Jay's eyes. "You're starting to understand."

"But not agreeing," Jay said. "I've not agreed

to anything." He paused as Malcolm pulled an envelope out of the inside pocket of his jacket. "I'm not signing anything, either."

"Just take a look at it," Malcolm said as he spread the contract on the table. He tugged a pen from the same pocket and placed it next to the contract. "Just read it through. Or not. It's your decision."

"*My* decision?"

"Of course," Malcolm said. "Always. But…"

"But you owe Frank," Jay said. "And Rhodium wants me gone…"

"And you will be gone if you don't sign." Malcolm paused for a second, catching his friend's eye as he waited for him to think it through. "The bonus alone will get you a house…"

"In California?"

"Wherever you want," Malcolm said. "But sure, California, if that's where you want to be." He paused again, before adding, "And there's healthcare, too. Comprehensive. Including family members."

Jay looked up.

"You could get a good place for your mom. I hear there's lots of good hospices in California, Jay. She could be really comfortable, you know?"

"Yeah…" Jay skimmed the first few lines of the contract.

"Health benefits are on page six," Malcolm said. "I'm going to step out. I'll get a pizza. I'll let you read in peace," he said. "But when I get back…"

"I'll sign it, I guess," Jay said.

"It's for the best, Jay." Malcolm stood up. "It really is."

Jay nodded. He flicked through the contract as Malcolm headed for the door. "Hey," he said, stopping Malcolm before he left the apartment."

"What?"

"No garlic? Okay?" Jay shrugged and said, "I don't do garlic."

"Sure," Malcolm said. He nodded at the contract. "Just make sure you sign it."

Jay reached for the pen, swore once, and then signed the last page.

"I'm going back to the fucking desert," he said and tossed the pen onto the table.

5

With each rung of the ladder, Haines imagined an increasingly bleak, musty, dusty, and damp bunker beneath the desert. It was, she mused, most likely a government depot, the intended contents of which some pen pusher from the BLM decided warranted a secret entrance and fifty feet or so of soil and rock above it.

"Either that or a survivalist's wet dream," she whispered as she climbed down another two rungs. The footwear she borrowed from Claud – as Beane called his partner – was surprisingly comfortable. And, as Haines reached the bottom rung of the ladder, she realised the bunker was too.

"Impressive, eh?" Beane said as he slid the last few feet with his boots on the outside of the rungs. He landed with a soft thump on the thick rubber mat at the foot of the ladder and then gently guided Haines to one side as Claud joined them. "You weren't expecting this, were you?"

"No," Haines said as she took in the space around the ladder. "I really wasn't."

"Then let me start the tour," Beane said. He waved Haines forward with a chivalrous roll of his hand and talked her through each section of the bunker. "If you're thinking BLM built this, then you'd be right," he said as they crossed the mats through a short space humming with the soft, almost inaudible, whir of the ventilation system. "It was built in the 50s as a Cold War bolthole. Then," Beane said, pausing to punch a code into a keypad to the right of what looked to Haines like a door from a nuclear submarine, "it was abandoned to everything but the snakes."

"Snakes?"

"Relax," Beane said as Haines shivered. "All gone now."

"Good," she said. "My daughter used to be fascinated by them, even had one in a glass thing in her room."

"A terrarium?"

"Yes," Haines said. "Something like that."

Bean gestured for her to step to one side, and then with a nod to Claud, he opened the door. The familiar sound of computer servers and fans drifted through the gap around the door until it was fully open and Beane nodded for Haines to step into a modern computer lab complete with bundles of cables snaked across the floor with small metal ramps and black and yellow hazard tape guiding staff and visitors around the maze of computer desks and server units. Haines frowned as the noise level rose as they stepped inside until Beane guided her to the first of three alcoves with heavy glass doors and walls cut into the rock. He waved to Claud, who closed the door behind them.

"She's not coming in?"

"She hasn't got the clearance," Beane said.

Haines turned and said, "So, she's just going to wait out there?"

"Until we're done." Beane nodded.

"And how long will that be?"

"Ah, sometime tomorrow morning."

"Tomorrow morning?" Haines stopped a few feet from the alcove. "No, that can't happen. I have a bunch of meetings…"

"They've been dealt with," Beane said.

"And my daughter…"

"Also…" Beane hesitated before saying, "dealt with, but in a much nicer way, I promise."

"What did you do?"

"Mr Adler made sure your husband, Bill, and your daughter, Tessa, were most comfortable at the resort…"

"Resort? What resort?"

"Well," Beane said, taking a step back as Glenn Adler followed a track between the hazard lines to greet them. "I'll let Mr Adler explain." Beane dipped his head at Adler, and then pointed at a small door cut into the rock in the opposite wall. "I'll be in the recreation room if you need me, Senator." He grinned and then walked away as Adler reached out to shake Haines' hand.

"You made it," he said, smiling as he let go of the senator's hand to open the alcove door. "We'll be comfortable in here and I can explain everything."

"Okay," Haines said. "I'd appreciate that."

She stepped into the alcove and took a seat on a generous, cushioned bench on the far side of a plain, clean, and sturdy table. Haines relaxed her shoulders as Adler shut the door and the hum and whir of the computers evaporated as he pulled up a chair to sit opposite her.

Adler pointed at the ceiling and the glass and said, "Noise reducing."

"It's quite a noise." Haines turned her head to glance at the computers, suddenly aware that the only people she had yet to see inside the bunker were Beane, Adler, and herself.

"And warm," Adler said. "Thank God for air conditioning."

"Yes," Haines said. She leaned forward. "Where is everyone?"

"*Everyone*?" Adler frowned. "You mean staff, perhaps?"

"I do." Haines pointed at the closest computer. "Who sits there, for example?"

"Oh, we have some tech people come down here every now and again, but this is really more of a remote site." He paused and said, "Think of it as a window into something larger. In fact..." Adler pushed his chair back and stood up. "Hold that thought until I find us some coffee and something to eat. I'll be right back."

Haines watched him leave and then stood to walk to the glass for a closer look at the bunker's interior. The screens were blank, but the familiar slow blink of a blue light in the corner of the screens facing her suggested they were in energy saver mode, waiting to be activated.

"Out of the dark," she whispered. "Like me."

The ceiling was low, but not as low as she might have imagined. Haines looked at the floor, half expecting to see old tyre tracks as she guessed the bunker could easily accommodate a heavy-duty military truck or two, squeezed in side by side. The computers filled the space between the rock walls, while the servers lined the walls opposite the alcoves. Haines opened the door for Adler when he returned and then sat down on the bench waiting to be brought out of *saver mode*. The thought made her smile and brought a frown to Adler's brow as he poured the coffee.

"You're amused," he said.

"I am."

"And comfortable?"

"As comfortable as I can be in a goldfish bowl, Glenn."

"Yes," he said. "It's rather austere, but I assure you the sleeping quarters are more comfortable."

"Sleeping quarters? How long am I going to be down here? And to what purpose? And what makes you think…"

"I don't," Adler said as he handed Haines a cup of coffee and a Danish on a square plate. "I don't *think* or even presume to think for you, Senator. Everything has been taken care of. Including your family."

"Yes, but…"

"And," Adler said, holding up a hand to stop Haines as he sat down, "all will be revealed very shortly. So, if you will, Warren. Try the coffee – it's Colombian."

"Yes, it's…" Haines took a sip and nodded. "Rich."

"Not too strong?"

"No," she said. "It's just right."

"I'm pleased." Adler poured a second cup and then pushed his chair back a little to make space for his legs as he crossed one over the other. Adler faced the door with his right knee resting against the edge of the table. "What I'm about to tell you," he said as he placed his cup on a saucer, "is above Beane's pay grade, and, frankly, above yours, too, Senator."

"Then why…"

"Please," Adler said. "I'll come to that. But let me start at the beginning." Adler reached for the coffee, then smiled and rested his hands in his lap instead. "You're familiar with WARCOM?"

"The Navy's Special Warfare Command?" Haines nodded. "Somewhat. But Utah is a little farther from the coast, Glenn."

"It is, but for the sake of acronyms, I mention it because you are currently sitting in the visitor alcove of WARDEV, a slightly more succinct acronym for Warfare Development. I've been heading WARDEV for many years now, and I can't tell you how many times I've had to beat off one general or another who wanted to add the word *special* or *future*, or some such to the program. Wholly unnecessary, and expensive when one thinks about all the changes that must be made to headed paper, and logos and such."

"Glenn?"

"Yes?" Adler looked up.

"You didn't bring me fifty feet underground to talk about stationary."

"No, I didn't," he said. "But I tell you this to help you understand that WARDEV has a very simple remit. We explore the development of war – now and in the near and far future. You sit on several committees in D.C. that have remote connections to the work of WARDEV, even if they don't know it. You're here to witness something tonight, and through the course of this adventure, in order to whisper in the ears of the right people at the right time, in order that these remotely connected bodies and committees make the right decisions when the time comes."

"Glenn, I…"

"You don't have to think about it at the present time," Adler said, cutting her off. "But I assure you, good things will happen in the fabulous state of Utah, for you and its businesses and residents, with favourable numbers of employment and investment that will put you in a good position if you ever chose to advance your political career, and maybe aim a little higher than you thought feasible or even possible."

"You're saying WARDEV has a war chest…"

"A sizeable one, yes."

"And could fund…"

"Discretely and through various means, a presidential campaign. Yes. That's what I'm saying. But…" Adler reached for his coffee, letting the promise of political capital simmer for a moment as he took a sip. He put the cup down with a slight clatter, muttering a soft *oops* before continuing. "But that's a side issue. I've brought you down here to give you a ringside seat to WARDEV's crowning achievement to date. Actually," he said, correcting himself. "It's something we hope will be a crowning achievement. It has yet to be tested."

"What has?"

"Project Reviver," Adler said. He gestured at the bunker on the other side of the glass. "You're looking at it. The data on these computers is air-gapped, but via a heavily encrypted satellite link, I will show you exactly what you need to know to understand Reviver, and, at least to a point, the potential benefits and ramifications of the project."

"These are just words, Glenn. You're toying with me. You need to break it down and give me something *before* you start wowing me with meaningless charts and simulations on your computers." Haines opened her palms and gave Adler a wide-eyed stare. "So far, I couldn't tell you what the fuck you're talking about. And until I know at least this much," she said, pinching her finger and thumb together. "Then this is a colossal waste of my time."

"But with good coffee," Adler said, disarming Haines with that easy smile of his she had noticed the first time they met.

"What?" Haines shook her head and then glanced at the coffeepot. "Yes. Sure. It's good. But Glenn…"

"Project Reviver is, in essence, a satellite delivery system that has been developed to beam a focused wave of ceti radiation onto the earth."

"It's a what? And what kind of radiation?"

"Ceti radiation," Adler said. "From space. Collected by…" He paused and waved his hand. "Never mind how it's collected and don't ask me *who* does the collecting. Just know that this radiation has remarkable properties that, when channelled on a controlled burst of gamma waves…"

"Gamma radiation?" Haines leaned back in her seat. She ran her fingers along the edge of the table and clutched it. "*That* I've heard of. It passes through stuff."

"It does," Adler said. "It passes through lots of *stuff*. But I can assure you. We are quite safe here."

"*Here*? As in inside *this* bunker?"

"Yes."

"You're aiming this satellite at the earth?"

"Above your head. Yes." Adler nodded.

"But why?"

"Well, firstly, and rather arrogantly, because we can. We have developed the means to do so. We have weaponised beams of directional radiation." Adler frowned. "That never comes out right." He uncrossed his legs, turned his chair to face Haines, and pushed his cup and saucer to one side. "I'm not talking about blasting people with radioactive gamma waves. Gamma waves are merely the delivery system for heavily ionised particles with the potential to regenerate, or *revive*, if you will, dead material."

"Material?"

"Dead cells, Senator."

"In the ground, or…"

"In a variety of things. So far we've developed – in a limited capacity, I must add – the means to revive dead cells in controlled laboratory situations. But we've always had grander plans, and I'll admit I have pushed for development of the delivery system, to the point where we can deliver the package…"

"The ceti radiation?"

"Yes," Adler said. "We can deliver it. We know what it *should* do. Now we just need to do it."

"Revive something?"

"Yes."

"Revive *what*, exactly?"

Adler leaned back in his chair and smiled. "Now *that* is above your pay grade. We'll call that Phase Two."

"And Phase One? What does that involve?"

Adler pointed at the ceiling. "Twenty square feet of desert. Right above your head."

"You're not serious?"

"I *am* serious, Senator. Because I need to show you that this technology is both safe and potentially hugely lucrative in so many markets. Honestly," he said, after a brief pause. "The possibilities are limitless."

"For reviving dead stuff?"

"Coral reefs. Old growth forest," Adler said, ticking things off on his fingers. "Even human cells. If we can target twenty square feet of desert from space, we can hit a micron of tissue in a human body in an operating theatre."

"With gamma radiation, Glenn. That's what you said."

"Yes, but only a little."

"Okay…" Haines sighed. "I guess I'm trapped in the bunker until the all clear." She looked at Adler and said, "When does the show start?"

"Senator Haines," Adler said with a smile. "It's already begun."

6

Adler, Haines discovered, was right about the sleeping quarters; they were comfortable. But even though the soft leather armchair and a nightcap from the well-stocked drinks cabinet was tempting, Haines spent much of the night at the worktable, drumming her fingers on the surface as she tried to get her head around what Adler had told her. She looked up at the rocky ceiling more often than she cared to admit, as she imagined the beam of whatever it was Adler had pointed at the patch of BLM ground searing the earth and frying her mind.

"It's not like that at all," Adler had said when they joined Beane in the recreation room for a passable microwave dinner. "The beauty of ceti radiation is the incredibly short half-life. We're talking hours. Literally. There's so much energy inside one particle, it's got one big bang – albeit on a micro scale – and then it's all over. It's the reason it's been so hard to discover."

"Who discovered it?"

"Doctor Chandler Green," Adler said. He winked at Beane as the security operative's lips spread in a faint smile. "An interesting man. Far more unstable than the radiation he's researching."

"How did he find it?"

"I'm not even sure he did," Adler said. "He hypothesized its existence based on data and observations that are far beyond my comprehension." Adler shrugged when Haines borrowed Beane's amused smile. "Hard to believe, eh? But that's not important. The key to this whole thing…" Adler gestured at the room, implying something grander, larger, and far beyond what Haines thought she could comprehend. "The whole project is based on the premise of what Green's hypothetical radioactive particles could do."

"Revive dead cells?"

"Exactly," Adler said. He paused as Beane stood up, nodding when he said it was Claud's turn to eat.

"Wait," Haines said. "I thought…"

"Beane told you she wasn't allowed inside?" Adler said as Beane walked away. "He probably said it with a straight face, too."

"He did," Haines said.

"Well…" Adler let the thought hang in the air, unfinished. "Back to Green," he said, after a short pause. "Whether the man fully appreciates the enormity of what he's uncovered doesn't really matter. That's my job. And, fortunately, I have the resources to dial up certain research areas of interest, and dial them down again if they prove to be a dead end."

Haines laughed and said, "You sound like a government philanthropist."

"I suppose I am," Adler said. "Although I

think you'll find it's *governments*. Plural." He smiled again. "But we'll come back to that. In the meantime, I think it's best we retire for the evening. If I'm right, and this works, then you'll be in a better position to grasp the results of the reviver project if you're well rested." He stood up and gathered his empty plate and utensils on a plastic tray. "Goodnight, Senator."

But Haines struggled to rest, and slept in short, fitful bursts of forty minutes here, another twenty there, until Beane knocked lightly on her door just after dawn.

"Time to go, Senator," he said, raising his voice slightly to pass through the door. "There's cinnamon rolls and coffee, if you're hungry."

"I'll be right there."

Haines ate breakfast alone as the rest of the team, together with a few new faces dressed in what Haines labelled *boffin attire*, bustled about the computers and screens, exchanging the occasional nod and what looked like relieved smiles as if the project had *actually worked* beyond what they might have thought up until the moment of truth.

Haines' moment of truth came when she followed Beane up the ladder to the surface. He stepped onto a shallow platform at the top to open the hatch and then gestured to Haines to be the first to go outside.

"It's safe?" she asked. "I mean, you're sure?"

"What you're really asking is if the US government really did just irradiate a patch of land outside Salt Lake City with radioactive space dust beamed to earth on waves of gamma radiation, without the consent of the people?"

"Well, when you put it like that," Haines said, suddenly conscious of the rungs of the ladder pressing into the soles of her feet.

"It's Grade A conspiracy level shit, isn't it, Senator?" Beane laughed as he popped the hatch. "After you, ma'am."

Haines tilted her head and blinked in the sunlight. She swore under her breath and then climbed the last few rungs of the ladder and stepped out of the tube.

"Easy now," Beane said. "That last step can be tricky."

It was, Haines discovered, but not as tricky as trying to put words to what she saw above ground. She stepped to one side to make room for Beane and whoever else was joining them, and then lifted her hand to her brow to protect her eyes from the glare of the early morning sun. The twenty-foot square patch of earth had been seared of life, making the surrounding scrub and earth looked tanned in comparison. But it wasn't burned – even though *burned* was exactly what Haines had pictured when she tried to imagine what she was going to see above ground. There was life poking out of the soil, and, while she was no botanist, the new shoots of vegetation were unusual. On closer inspection, as she knelt at the very edge of the test area – not quite ready to step inside it – they seemed tougher, and *older* somehow.

"This is what we expected," Adler said,

surprising her with his voice as she thought he was still down below. "The combination of the gamma waves and the ceti radiation have a detrimental effect on living tissue, while…" He paused to inspect a sturdy shoot in front of Haines. "…reviving and accelerating the growth of dead matter."

"What is that?" Haines said, pointing at the shoot. "I don't recognise it." She paused, adding, "And is it growing? I mean, is it growing *that fast*, as we're watching it?"

"It appears so," Adler said. "Ah, Dr Green, if only you could see this for yourself."

"Good point," Haines said. "Why isn't he here?"

"Senator," Adler said as she stood up. "Dr Green works best in a more remote capacity. He fuels his research with an interesting, if a little alarming, range of stimulants. In short," Adler said with a smile. "He's not fit for fieldwork."

"But you'll…" Haines stopped talking as Beane clicked his fingers to get Adler's attention.

"You found it, Jim?"

"Yeah, I'm pretty sure," Beane said. He pointed at the ground in front of him, about five feet inside the square. "This is where I buried him."

"Buried *who*?" Haines asked as she followed Adler inside the test area.

"Chester's puppy," Beane said.

"What?"

"Senator," Adler said. "The purpose of this test was to show you the potential of, and, more importantly, the control we have over the Reviver delivery vehicle."

"The satellite?"

"Exactly." Adler nodded. "By showing you the degree of control we have on our own soil… Case in point," he said, gesturing at the test square of seared but strangely vibrant ground. "Then, having seen the results for yourself, you'll be in a much better position to champion our cause. However…" Adler gestured at the ground in front of Beane. Haines squinted in the sunlight as the soil appeared to tremble. "While we can't know exactly what's beneath the surface, and at what depth, without doing a survey and likely drawing the attention of the good people of Vernon. We can hedge our bets and experiment with test subjects of our own."

"Chester's puppy?" Haines said.

"Right," Beane said as he settled into a crouch. "I may have mentioned Chester's big floppy ears, but I never got as far to tell you she's a mother. Chester had a litter of puppies – six in all – and one of them died a couple of months later. The vet said it was a virus. We buried Mable…" Beane looked up and grinned. "The twins gave her the name."

"Okay."

"So we buried Mable in a shoebox in the backyard. I dug her up a few days ago and moved her out here."

"Still in the box?"

"No," Beane said, shaking his head. "Just beneath the surface. Maybe twelve inches." He scratched at the ground with the small trowel, giving Haines the impression, she was on some crazy archaeological dig. Only the bones they were looking for were – and this was the part she struggled with – reanimated.

"It's tempting to think we're playing god," Adler said as Beane set the trowel to one side and dug his hands into the soil. "And I would be the first to agree that, in a sense, that's exactly what we're doing." He smiled as Haines gasped at the sight of Mabel pressing her paws into the hole Beane had just excavated.

"Why didn't she suffocate?" Haines said. "I mean…"

"Timing," Adler said. "We applied the data from the lab and then took a guess at the length of time it would take the ceti particles to work their magic." He checked his watch. "What was it we said, Beane?"

"About half an hour per inch," Beane said. "Something like that." He widened the hole and laughed as Mabel stuck her snout out of the ground to take her second first breath of air. "Just wait until the twins see you."

"They can't, of course," Adler said. "As discussed."

"Sure," Beane said, although Haines caught the pinch of disappointment in his voice. Haines watched as Beane cleaned the puppy up and then collected Mabel in his arms. "I'll get her some water," he said and excused himself.

Adler waited until Beane was gone, and said, "As you can see, this is heady stuff."

"It is," Haines said. "But what possible application could WARDEV envisage for reanimation?"

"*Revival*, Senator," Adler said. "Reviving dead cells." He smiled as Beane presented the puppy to Claud, and her otherwise professional exterior cracked with an expression of joy that only a puppy can bring. "Beyond the obvious benefits of bringing things back to life – including the health benefits, once we get this approved."

"Human trials?"

"Oh, we're not there yet, Senator," Adler said. "It will be a vigorous and lengthy process – perhaps even decades before we hear about the first breakthroughs in the medical application of ceti radiation. The particles are piggybacking something far more toxic, after all." Adler fell silent as Mabel's head flopped to one side in Claud's arms. "While ceti can revive cells, some creatures won't survive the gamma radiation. Mabel is simply not robust enough."

"Not robust?" Haines looked at Adler. "So the medical application…"

"Is decades into the future. As I said."

"Actually, Glenn," Haines said. "You haven't said very much at all. I still don't know what WARDEV wants with this technology. I can't begin to imagine what you can possibly get out of it, beyond scorching patches of earth and sprouting new life. I mean, is that it?" Haines said, suddenly convinced *Reviver* was a weapon. "Did you weaponize a satellite? Only you've dressed it up as something else?"

"It might seem so," Adler said. "And I admit it is tempting to think we could *scorch* – as you put it – strategic parts of the battlespace. But conventional weapons do that already, and at a fraction of the cost. This," he said, gesturing at the boundaries of the test area. "Is a multi-billion-dollar square of land. Twenty-square feet, to be exact. Now, while we can scale up the test area significantly..."

"No," Haines said with a shake of her head. "Don't even begin to tell me you're thinking of scaling this up."

"Not in America," Adler said. "Of course not. But scaling up *is* part of WARDEV's plans for the Reviver Project. But until we're ready to take that next step, I'm afraid it's all rather hypothetical."

"You said this whole thing was a hypothesis," Haines said. She turned to look at Beane as he pointed at the puppy and shook his head. "You took Green's idea and built a weapon out of it."

"A weapon limited in scope and far too costly to deploy. No, Senator," Haines said. He gripped her gently to guide her out of the square of what Haines dubbed *scorched land*. "There are other applications, but they will have to wait. But now you've seen what Reviver can do, I think you'll agree that the potential applications have moved beyond the hypothetical. Reviver works, Warren. And it can work for both of us. I'd like you to remember that as we move forward."

Adler said nothing more, and Haines didn't

ask. But neither did she turn around for one last look at the ground, the new, hardy, once dead shoots of vegetation drinking in the sun, and the tremors of sand, rattling as if they were bouncing on the skin of a drum, as more dead life clawed its way out of the earth.

7

Whisky had never been Luci's drink of choice, but somewhere between graduating from the University of East Anglia with an MSci in Geology and taking her PhD in Palaeontology at the University of Manchester – just up the road from the parents in Churlington Hawley, Joci had decided that, if Luci was going to continue *graduating with stuff*, then they needed a tradition to celebrate with.

"Our *own* tradition," she had said before Luci even thought about mentioning the parents. "We can celebrate with them for sure, but we need something just for us. Whatever you like. But just us. Okay?"

Joci hadn't mentioned celebrating any of her achievements, but then Joci rarely talked about her own career path, and neither did their parents.

"Professional Adventurer just doesn't seem to be a thing," Joci had said after another *serious talk* with their parents the night Luci defended her PhD in what Joci called *another obscure something or other about dead stuff*. She said it with a smile, followed up by the usual heartfelt hug and breathy whisper of adoration and love, congratulating her younger sister on yet another *important piece of paper*. Joci's important pieces of paper were usually permits, some of which were just as difficult to obtain as Luci's degrees.

But between discussing the merits of the more obscure permits Joci had *obtained*, as she put it, Luci discovered exactly where, if not how, they should have their ritual.

"In the thunderbox," she said. "At the bottom of the garden."

The outside lavatory was a relic from wartime England, and a secret refuge for the twins when they wanted to hide from their parents, or simply hide things. The shed rattled with every train that thundered past, sending the younger Hamptons into fits of giggles as dust tumbled onto them from above as the walls shook, and Joci, then Luci, screamed at the top of their lungs, confident that no one would hear them.

And so it was the night before their parents drove them to the airport. The twins snuck out of the house when their parents were in bed, and shared a small bottle of Jack Daniels – Joci's contribution to the tradition.

"It's not like it's my favourite," she said. "Only that it's cheap, and in every country I've ever been, I can almost guarantee there's a bottle of Jack in some bar, or someone's truck." She shrugged, took a sip, and then handed the bottle to Luci. "But this place gets smaller every time we sneak in here."

"Except," Luci said, wiping her mouth with the back of her hand. "We really don't have to sneak anymore, Joci."

"No?" Joci took the bottle when Luci handed it to her. "You don't see Dad's nervous tic when we have a glass of wine at dinner? Or what about Mum? What would she say if you started smoking?"

"But I don't smoke." Luci frowned as Joci fished a crumpled packet of cigarettes out of her jeans.

"Share one with me?" Joci said.

"Since when did you smoke?"

Joci lit the cigarette and shrugged. "Since one long, boring, and *hot* container ship too many."

Luci watched her sister take the first drag on her cigarette and wondered how different their lives had become. She, the early achiever, jumping ahead two years to study and graduate youngest in every class. And Joci – just six minutes older, but already worldly wise, and a consummate liar. She took the cigarette when Joci handed it to her, then took a careful pull on it, knowing she would cough, that she would choke, and that she would hate it. But knowing too that the smile on her sister's face would be worth it.

And then they felt the first rumble of an approaching train.

"Ready?" Joci said as Luci coughed.

"Yes..."

Luci held the cigarette to one side, then grinned at Joci from her side of the toilet. The twins tipped their heads back against the sides of the shed, and, when the train reached them and the shed began to shake, they screamed at the top of their lungs, faltering halfway through the train's passage when they realised it was a freight train, only to scream again when they recovered.

Joci took a slug of whisky, then pinched the cigarette from Luci's fingers. She smoked as Luci sipped. The train rumbled into the night and Joci kicked the door open for some air. The twins caught each other's eye and grinned.

"I'm going to miss you," Joci said.

"I know."

"You *know*?"

"Yes," Luci said. "You say the same thing every time. That you're *going to miss me* and, in a minute, you'll say something like *next time, Luci, you should come with me*, even though you know I never will."

"You're so smart," Joci said. She clamped the cigarette between her lips and reached out, waggling her fingers until Luci gave her the bottle."

"I am," Luci said.

"Then tell me why you won't come with me?"

"Because…" Luci sighed as she thought about it. "Because your kind of adventure isn't my kind. What you do can be dangerous."

"And digging in Libya isn't?"

"I'm with a team of archaeologists from a respected university."

"And that makes you safe, does it?"

"I think it does," Luci said with a nod.

"And yet…" Joci paused for a last puff of the cigarette before flicking the butt into the garden. "You still told the folks you're going to Mojave?"

"The invite is from Cal State. They have a field station in the Mojave Desert. I'm just going to a different desert. It's not a stretch, Joci."

"You don't think so?" Joci laughed. "But it's still a lie."

"A little one." Luci laughed as Joci rolled her eyes. "I know. I get it. Here we are, twenty-six years old, telling lies to our parents and hiding in the shed at the bottom of the garden…"

"Drinking and smoking," Joci said.

"Like a couple of teenagers."

"Yep." Joci nodded. "That's about right." She looked at her sister and said, "Do we need therapy? Or do they?"

"They do," Luci said, without hesitation. "Definitely."

The night drifted into stories about Joci's tangle of twisted relationships, Luci's struggles with peers and peer reviews in the snobbish and chauvinistic world of academia, interjected with screaming at trains and sipping the last dregs of whisky.

"You know," Joci said, once the bottle was finished and the thunderbox had cooled to the point of being decidedly uncomfortable. "We're looking for the same thing. You in the desert at the top of Africa, and me in the jungle, somewhere in the middle."

"We are?"

"We're looking for big beasts, sis. The difference is," Joci said as she stood up. "Yours are dead."

"But you're looking for something, too?"

Luci stood up and slid her hand through the crook of Joci's arm as they wandered back up the garden to the house. The first fingers of dawn plucked at the sky, and the two young women yawned at the thought of packing and pretending they were well rested. "What is it you're looking for?"

"A rumour," Joci said. "Or the whisper of something that might be a rumour, or a myth, but is ultimately treasure waiting to be found. Remember that magazine I told you about?"

"What *Guns & Ammo*? Or," Luci said, laughing as Joci protested. "Wait for it… *Pinups & Pushups!*" Luci stopped for a round of spontaneous and unstoppable giggling.

"You finished?"

"Yeah," Luci said, wiping her eyes. "I might have made that last one up."

"You think?"

"Yes…" Luci took a deep breath. "I'm fine. I'm ready." She waved at her sister. "Just talk. I'll listen."

"Okay," Joci said, giving Luci another minute. "I pitched the idea for an article to *National Geographic*. They were interested, but then I heard nothing. So while I waited, and waited, a friend of mine pitched the same idea, on my behalf, and without me knowing, to *Outside Magazine*."

"I've heard of *both* of them," Luci said.

"I'd be worried if you hadn't, But, *both* magazines got into a bit of a fight over it, and it went to some kind of auction, or an editors' agreement, and… Well, either way, sis, I've got the money, and I've got the promise of one magazine publishing the story, and the other gets first dibs on the second article."

"I don't understand," Luci said. "Are they both going to publish?"

"No." Joci shook her head. "But it turns out both magazines like the idea of some young, blonde, British girl wandering into the jungle in search of a mythical beast that might or might not be a dragon."

"And they want photos of the same *young…blonde…*"

"Sure," Joci said. "But I send the X-rated ones to *Pinups & Pushups*." Joci forced a fake frown onto her brow as she said, "Dad doesn't still subscribe to that one, does he?"

"Probably," Luci said. She took a moment to study her sister, smiling as it really was like looking in a mirror, and it never got old. Then Luci reached for Joci's hand. "You will be careful, won't you?"

"Always," Joci said. "Now come here. Give me a hug." Joci pulled Luci close, held her tight, and then sniffed her hair. "You stink of cigarettes, girl. Better go shower before breakfast."

"*I* stink?" Luci pulled her head back to stare at her sister and then leaned in again to kiss her on the cheek. "I'll miss you," she said.

"I know." Joci nodded and then gestured at the house. "Go on ahead of me. I need to make a call."

"Okay," Luci said.

She took the empty bottle and waggled it between her fingers, mouthing the word *recycling* before walking back to the house. She placed the bottle quietly into the bin for glass, sniffed the sleeve of her fleece jacket and wrinkled her nose as she discovered Joci was right; she stank of cigarettes. Luci took one last look at her sister, waved, and then slipped inside the house.

Breakfast *happened* a few hours later, to the tune of Beth Hampton's concerns about how tired *her girls* looked, together with Joshua Hampton's clock-watching and *leaving in ten minutes* followed by *now leaving in five minutes*, until they were all packed, out of the house, and in the Mini on the way to the airport. Mr Hampton took the motorway, cursing the traffic and reminding *his girls* about how important it was to factor the unexpected into all plans and every aspect of life.

"And he wonders why he never gets a promotion?" Joci whispered to Luci on the backseat.

While Luci might have wondered how they would check in to their different flights without revealing their true destinations, the new parking fares that stacked up ridiculously by the minute prompted Joshua Hampton to suggest saying goodbye at the car.

"Oh, Josh, we can't," Beth had said.

But *the girls* were surprisingly willing to do just that, and they breezed into departures with the feeling of success tempered with a lack of sleep, too much whisky, and, in Luci's case, a sore throat from smoking and screaming.

Hours later, following a more tearful goodbye than she had anticipated, Luci finally boarded her flight to Heathrow, from where she would fly to Marseille, France, and then on to Carthage, Tunisia, before one last hop to land in Misrata International Airport in the Mediterranean coastal city of the same name in Libya. Luci had been warned that the final leg of her journey would be hot and exhausting as she drove the last twenty hours from the coast through the desert to the Cal State camp.

"Sleep on the plane, honey," Sugar Albuquerque, the fifty-three-year-old expedition leader, had told her when they had talked before the flight. "Jamillah and Fahd will take good care of you, but it's a bumpy ride. Sleep when you can."

Luci guessed that *bumpy rides* were part and parcel of each and every one of Joci's adventures, and she looked forward to swapping stories the very next time they met.

"Until then," she whispered, setting aside a worn, much annotated copy of *The Rubáiyát of Omar Khayyám*, to catch a few hours' sleep.

Luci's chin slumped to her chest just five minutes after her Heathrow departure.

8

After two long days in Washington, D.C. Haines had almost forgotten the events of the previous week in the bunker just outside the tiny town of Vernon. She took a cab from Salt Lake City International Airport, calling ahead to let Bill know she would be late – *again*, that they should go ahead and eat and she'll join them for coffee.

"Yes, I know Tessa is pissed at me for missing everything. You don't have to remind me every time, Bill. Remember, you signed on for this," Haines said from the backseat of the cab. She switched her smartphone to her right ear, half listening to her husband as the cab driver tried to get her attention. "Hold on, Bill. I'll call you back." Haines leaned forward to better hear what the driver had to say.

"There's three of them," he said, pointing at the big, black SUV slowing in front of the cab, the one on the left, and a third on the right. "They've got me boxed in." The cabbie turned to look at Haines, and the wild look in his eyes sent a tremor of panic through her body. "Is this a kidnapping?" the cabbie said. "Are they terrorists?"

Haines took a breath, lifted her head and peered over the dash to try to read the plates on the car in front. "I don't think so," she said, adding, "I'm a senator. This is probably something to do with me."

"Then I should pull over?"

"Yes," Haines said. And then, when the driver of the SUV on the right lowered her window, and Claud pointed at the breakdown lane, Haines nodded. "Definitely. You should stop." She fumbled some cash out of her briefcase and paid the driver for his trouble as soon as he slowed the cab to a stop. Haines had barely closed the passenger door before he pulled away. "Hey! You've got my overnight bag in the trunk!"

"Claud will send someone for it," Beane said as he joined her. "Let me take your briefcase." He reached for it, but Haines pulled it away from him. "Ma'am?"

"First," Haines said. "Tell me what's going on."

Beane hesitated, glancing left and right until he realised an open highway with the sound of passing vehicles was as secure a space to talk as any. "It's Vernon," he said.

"The town?"

"Yes, ma'am."

Haines sighed and said, "Tell me this isn't about the puppy, Beane."

"Honestly, Senator, I wish it was. But there's something else going on up there, and, well, I can't get hold of Adler. And I need someone at least remotely connected to the project…"

"Go on," Haines said, almost amused when she noticed Beane didn't say the name *Reviver* out loud.

"There's been a sighting of something."

"*Something?*"

"It's pretty big, ma'am."

"And you think it has something to do with Adler's space rays and your dead puppy?" Haines laughed. "You don't need a senator, Beane. You should call *National Enquirer*, if it still exists."

"That's the thing," Beane said. "Somebody did."

"What?"

Beane nodded. "Some kid called Michael spotted what he said is a Utahraptor…"

"A *what?*"

"A dinosaur, ma'am," Beane said. "Nineteen feet long. The magazine called one of their experts. And, well, I've got a palaeontologist called Pat Carter combing the area with a bunch of enthusiasts, two missing dogs, three dead chickens, and a cat called Mumbles that's been missing for three days."

"Beane…"

"I shit you not," Beane said. "Honestly, I wish I was making this up. But that's not the worst of it."

"There's more?"

Beane nodded again. "There's a blood trail. A local found it. He's a friend of a friend, and he reached out."

"You mean we caught a break?" Haines said, as she caught the subtle change in Beane's demeanour.

"A little one," Beane said. "I've got a small

team of three following the trail. They called in just under an hour ago to confirm they had eyes on a large beast of some description. It looks sick. But they said it also looked powerful. I told them to hang back. They've got it corned."

"Cornered?"

"In a gully with a steep wall at one end, and my team at the other."

"No locals?"

"Not yet," Beane said with a shake of his head. He waited for a moment and then said, "How do you want to play it?"

"Me?"

"Senator…" Beane dipped his head as if deferring to his superior officer. "I've kept local law enforcement at arm's length for now. I had to pull a few strings. But the project is so far off the charts, it's not like they would recognise anyone in the chain of command, anyway. But a senator…"

"No, Beane." Haines took a step backward, stopping when Beane reached out to grip her arm, reminding her she was on the highway, as if the thought of taking responsibility for a living dinosaur made her forget. "I can't get involved."

"I'm just asking you to show your face in the local police station, grab a coffee, talk shit about the weather, and casually drop in the fact that you're authorising me and my team to take care of this peculiar situation."

"Peculiar? Beane? Really?"

"Well, Senator," he said. "I don't know what the hell else to call it. But the cops will be too busy filling in NDAs to worry about what's going on in mountains."

"And what will be going on in the mountains, Beane?"

Beane shrugged and said, "I guess we're hunting a dinosaur." He laughed, adding, "That'll be a first."

"For both of us," Haines said. "We'll look in on the cops, but then I'm coming with you. If Claud has a pair of shoes I can borrow?"

"Yes, ma'am." Beane gestured at Claud's SUV. "I'm sure she does."

Beane settled Haines in the back of Claud's vehicle, and then jogged to the lead SUV. The three black vehicles pulled off the shoulder a few seconds later and accelerated as one to begin the two, almost three-hour drive to Vernon.

Haines dealt with the local cops in less time than it took to pour three paper cups of what had to be the worst coffee she had tasted in a month. Claud handed out the NDAs while Haines promised to send over a box of her new favourite coffee.

"Something from Colombia," she said as she thanked the police officers for their good work and hoped they would find Mumbles the cat soon. "Don't ever make me do that again," she said once they were back in Claud's SUV.

"I'll try not to," Beane said. He gave Claud the coordinates for the team that had tracked the raptor into the mountains, and she punched them into the GPS mounted on the dash. Beane rode in the back with Haines, pressing assorted pieces of kit onto her lap as they drove.

"What's this?" Haines said as Beane lay a heavy vest on her legs. "Body armour?"

"Yes, ma'am." Beane caught Haines' eye as she fell silent. "You want Claud to take you back to the police station?"

"No," Haines said. "God no. I just didn't think we were going into battle."

"If I thought we were, then I would have left you in Vernon," Beane said. "But truthfully? I have no idea what we're getting into. I don't think anyone does. And that's the whole point, isn't it?"

"Yes…" Haines swallowed and then fell silent for a moment. She watched Beane slide a large pistol into a holster on his thigh and then looked through the gap between the seats to see lights up ahead. "Is that your team?"

"Not the trackers, ma'am," Claud said as she slowed to bump the SUV onto a rough track. "Those are the two SUVs from the highway. Beane sent them away when you were inside with the cops." Claud tilted the rear-view mirror to look at Haines. "Didn't want a *Men in Black* photo op for the National Enquirer."

"No," Haines said. "We don't want that."

"We'll be there in just a minute, ma'am," Claud said. She moved the mirror back to its original position and concentrated on the last mile of the drive into the mountains. Haines watched the scrub speed past on her right before turning back to Beane.

"Where is Adler, anyway?"

"High-level meetings with WARDEV,"

Beane said.

"And you couldn't get hold of him?"

"The kind of meetings WARDEV has are held in a sensitive compartmented information facility." Beane smiled and said, "Also called a SCIF. There's no signal in or out, and Adler's meetings tend to take a little longer than your usual meeting."

"A SCIF?" Haines frowned. "I've heard of them."

"And you've been in one." Beane jerked his thumb over his shoulder in the direction of Vernon. "The bunker."

"Really?"

"Yes, ma'am." Beane stopped talking as Claud slowed the SUV to a stop with the sound of gravel crunching under the SUV's thick tyres. "Right," Beane said as Claud got out of the vehicle. "House rules."

"What rules?"

"Senator…" Beane gestured at the trail leading into the mountains. "You're in my house now. My rules."

"Okay."

"You're going to walk between me and Claud. She'll be behind you. If I stop, you stop. You don't ask questions. In fact, you don't talk at all."

"Beane…"

"My job, Senator," he said, cutting her off. "Is to protect you. I have teams shadowing you to and from D.C., and on the ground in the city." He grinned as Haines' jaw dropped. "But this is new territory. Unknown, and, honestly, against my better judgement. But I think you need to see this as much as I do. And if this is a dinosaur... I mean, if that's even possible. Then it's like what Adler said back at the bunker. If you're going to support this project, then you need to know how safe it is."

"And how dangerous," Haines said.

"Yes, ma'am. That's what I was thinking."

"But it's not all you're thinking, Beane, is it?" Haines said as Beane fell silent.

Beane let out a sigh and said, "I'm thinking – off the record – that Adler and the folks up at WARDEV are playing god with their little big bang particles."

"Yes?"

"And if anyone was ever going to stop them, it won't be someone like me." Beane pointed at Haines' chest and said, "That'll be your job, Senator."

"If it comes to that..."

Beane nodded and then opened the passenger door when Claud knocked on it. "Gear up, Senator," Beane said as he stepped out into the cool night air.

Haines took the boots Claud handed her and quickly switched footwear. Claud helped her into the vest, explained the purpose of the ceramic plates, but admitted they might not do much against teeth.

"Teeth?" Haines said.

"I've seen *Jurassic Park*, ma'am," Claud said. "Between you and me?" Claud leaned in close to Haines and lowered her voice to a conspiratorial whisper. "These vests won't do shit against a raptor. If you'll pardon my French, ma'am."

"You're pardoned," Haines said. She forced a smile onto her lips and then turned to Beane as he presented her with a helmet.

"These funny things on top are night vision goggles," he said as he secured the helmet on Haines' head. "You'll get used to them."

"Now I feel like *I'm* in the movies," Haines said with a nod at Claud.

"Yes, ma'am," Beane said. "Just don't let it go to your head."

Haines promised she wouldn't and then said nothing for a few minutes as Beane and Claud grabbed automatic rifles from the rear of the SUV. She thought about what Claud had said about vests versus teeth and wondered what small bullets would do against the dinosaurs *she* remembered seeing in the same movie. But before she could ask Beane if he thought they might need something bigger, he tapped her on the shoulder, reminded her of his *house rules* and then led the way along the track. Haines followed a few seconds later, keeping the ten feet of distance between them that Beane had told her to, while lifting her head up to peer beneath the goggles, when she suddenly felt claustrophobic.

"Just lift them out of the way, ma'am," Claud said as she caught up. "Like this."

"Thank you," Haines said, as Claud clicked the goggles into the upright position, leaving

Haines free to squint into the darkness instead. "Do we even need night vision?" she asked, wondering if dinosaurs would react to flashlights.

"No idea," Claud said. "Just follow Beane."

"Right," Haines said.

They walked another half mile, pausing to give Haines a breather every five minutes as the trail inclined sharply. And then for a longer pause as a dark figure approached from the shadows wearing gear similar to theirs, but with a sense of urgency that immediately put Haines on edge.

"It's just ahead," the man said, pitching his voice barely above a whisper. "It's a mean-looking fucker. Never seen anything like it."

"Has it attacked?" Beane asked. "Is it aggressive?"

"No, sir," the man said. "Honestly, it's possible that it's dead already. It hasn't moved. But it's dug in like a tick between the rocks. We've got to get closer if we're going to do anything, Boss. But, honestly, I have no idea *what* we can do."

"Okay, Steve," Beane said. "Keep an eye on the senator. I'll take it from here."

Beane started down the trail, only to stop when Haines called out his name.

"I'm coming with you, Beane," she said.

"Ma'am…"

"No," she said. "You said it back in the SUV. I have to see this if I'm going to do anything about it."

"We're talking about a cornered, potentially wounded or sick beast about the size of a station wagon, ma'am. That right there is a combination from hell."

"Yes," Haines said. "It sounds like it. But if it's from hell, and if it's a result of the project, then *we* brought it here. We dragged it out of hell, and if I'm going to speak for or against that, then…" Haines opened her arms, saying nothing, as if Beane should finish her sentence for her.

"Then you need to see it," he said. "I get it." Beane waved Haines forward and then tilted his head to look at Claud. "You've got our six," he said.

Claud dipped her head. "Always."

Beane turned to Steve and said, "Hold the perimeter. If it runs, you bring it down. That's your priority. Whatever happens to us, you stop the thing first. Understood?"

"Yes, boss."

"Good." Beane slapped Steve on the shoulder. "Then let's do this." He led the way down the track, with Haines and Claud close behind him.

Haines glanced at the men and women with automatic rifles arranged in an arc halfway down the gully. The sides of the mountain sucked whatever light there was out of the gully and Haines fiddled her night vision goggles back into place, deciding it was better to be claustrophobic than blind. Of course, when Beane pressed the palm of his hand to her vest to stop her and then pointed at something a few feet in front of them, Haines wondered if it might not have been better to be blind after all?

"Do you see it?" Beane whispered, his breath warm against Haines' ear.

She nodded.

Even in the grainy green image produced by the goggles, the Utahraptor was an impressive sight. Haines watched the raptor's chest rise and fall and found her own breathing slipping into the same rhythm the longer they observed it. While its body was partially concealed by the rocks, Haines thought she could see an arm. It had feathers which surprised her, claws which horrified her, and teeth that confirmed what Claud had suggested back at the SUV that body armour would be next to useless if the raptor tried to bite them.

"I think it's dying," Beane whispered. "It's nearly over."

What was it Adler had said? That the puppy wasn't robust enough to survive the radiation once it had been revived? Wasn't this beast robust? Haines took a breath, nodding when Beane pointed out the raptor's shallow, rapid breathing, the sickly looking eyes, and then, when a lick of wind drifted down the gully, the smell of decay and death that came with it.

"It's a goner," Claud said, as she joined them. "Senator?"

"Yes?"

"I can take you home now," Claud said.

"No," Haines said. "I want to stay for a while." She looked at Beane and he nodded.

"That's fine, ma'am," he said. "We'll stay as long as you like."

Haines found a flat rock to sit on and made herself comfortable. However absurd or unlikely it was to sit a stone's throw away from a dying dinosaur, she knew she would wait as long as it took for the beast to return to the earth she had unwittingly wrestled it out of.

"I'll get some coffee," Claud said once the raptor stopped breathing.

9

Glenn Adler sat in a leather and wood chair that screamed Scandinavian design and leafed through a financial magazine from the coffee table in front of him as if he was waiting in the swanky outer office of a high end medical consultancy. But one look at the corrugated metal walls of the SCIF container dispelled the illusion, and neither the chairs, the magazines, nor the echo of the air-conditioning unit droning through the tiny waiting area could disguise the fact that he was sitting inside a shipping container while the WARDEV powers-that-be decided if they were ready to speak to him. It was a good question with a complicated answer. Adler would be the first to admit the project was over budget on an unprecedented scale, and without private investors, the budget would continue to grow out of proportion to the expected results that few could imagine, and even fewer would believe even if they had sufficient imagination.

There was nothing wrong with Adler's imagination.

As he entered his sixth decade on earth, Adler has lost track of the number of times people had commented on what they called his overactive mind. It had been confused with optimism on more than one occasion, but in both instances, Adler had chosen not to comment and not to correct people's opinions on how his brain worked. But when given the task of imagining the future of war, Adler had done just that. Which was why, when the secretary stepped out of the SCIF's inner meeting room, Adler was confident he had done nothing wrong, and had at no time stepped beyond the bounds of his remit. WARDEV had hired him for his imagination. Adler's only disappointment was that WARDEV lacked enough of the same to understand what it was he was suggesting, and how it could be applied.

Adler tossed the magazine onto the pile in front of him, stood up, straightened his jacket and tie, and followed the secretary to the door. He stepped inside and the secretary closed the door behind him, leaving Adler in the room with three other people, each of whom he knew personally, for better or worse.

"Have a seat Glenn," said the woman seated at the end of a long, narrow table. "Grab some coffee."

"Thanks, Rose," Adler said. He poured a cup of strong, black coffee from a freshly brewed pot, and sat down at the opposite end of the table with Rose Connelly – no title – the stubbornly successful forty-something the President of the United States trusted to make the right decisions in matters he neither wanted nor legally could be a part of. Rose dressed like she talked, with a casual abruptness, and the odd splash of colour on a shirt collar, for example, that might suddenly leap out at you when she pitched a particularly nasty question.

To her right, Adler's left, was Lieutenant Pete *Cold Fish* Bradley, a relatively low-ranked Navy SEAL with a huge amount of experience that made the relatively high-ranked officers above him nervous. It didn't surprise Adler when Bradley was given a liaison post with WARDEV. In Adler's opinion, the muscle-bound operator, almost half Adler's age, was welcome, as was anyone able to combine theoretical applications of actual tactics and material to future conflicts. That Bradley didn't want to be there was another matter, and not even close to being Adler's problem.

The woman on Connelly's left, however, was a whole other matter.

Major Takayo *Shooter* Ehle was an army ex-sniper with a keen situational awareness that often cut through Adler's charm and forced him to go over things *one more time* and one more time after that, until Ehle was sure she understood what Adler was talking about, and could separate his bluff, bluster, and bullshit from what she and Bradley comfortably called *actionable intel*. In other words, the truth, which was where things usually became difficult.

Ehle was an attractive woman, with a slight build she had maintained through her later years, making her – in Adler's mind, at least – a good match, if he ever needed a wingman when attending a political social event designed to curry favour for WARDEV. She was, with her long black hair, Connelly's complete opposite, both in looks and build. But both women possessed sharp minds and even sharper tongues. Adler guessed he was about to receive a tongue lashing, and the amused look on Bradley's face gave him an idea that it was imminent.

"How's the coffee, Glenn?" Connelly asked.

"It's just fine, *Rose*."

Adler appreciated the preamble, however briefly, as it gave him a moment to anticipate the first volley, for when it came, the attack would be relentless.

"Let's talk about Vernon," Connelly said.

"We can do that."

"Would you call it a success?"

Adler took a sip of coffee as Connelly pressed her hands flat on the table and tilted her head to one side to fix him with her piercing blue eyes.

"We conducted our first narrow beam delivery of the ceti particles from the Reviver platform in orbit," Adler said. He put his cup down on the table. "The parameters were set for a twenty square foot section of desert, directly above the Vernon bunker, at a depth of twenty inches. Of course, we know the gamma rays and some residual ceti particles will penetrate to a depth greater than twenty inches, but at no danger to the occupants of the bunker."

"Including Senator Warren Haines of Utah?"

"Yes," Adler said with a nod. "Senator Haines was present, as per our agreement."

"You explained the project to her?"

"I gave her the basics – the absolute minimum of information she needed to understand what we were doing."

"And why you were doing it?"

"No," Adler said. "Nothing more than potential applications in medicine, the treatment of dead cells, and a general, rather vague nod to the use of the Reviver beam as a weapon."

"I think it's an unnecessary risk," Ehle said. "To bring in a politician at this level, at this stage in the project."

"We had to bring one in at some point, Major," Adler said. "Haines' candidacy for anything greater than senator is currently weak, but it could also tip the other way with sufficient help. Utah had the requisite resources necessary for this test, and I brought her in as an asset." Adler looked around the room and said, "To which all of you consented. And," he added, turning to face Connelly, "you even cleared with those higher up the food chain."

Connelly held his gaze for a second and then switched track.

"Tell us about Dr Green."

"He's still on the payroll."

"And is he lucid?"

Adler played dumb and shook his head. "You'll have to explain."

"Damn it, Glenn," Connelly said, raising her voice. "He's a loose cannon and you know it. Green spends half his time drugged up to the eyeballs. One of these days, he's either going to mouth off to the wrong person at precisely the wrong time or take a swan dive from his New York balcony."

"Either of which scenario presents no problem to us, to WARDEV, or to Reviver," Adler said. "We've been through this…" He glanced at Ehle. "Countless times."

"And each time," Ehle said. "You fail to convince us why you need Green, and why, if you need him so badly, you don't do more to protect us from Green and to protect Green from himself."

"Because," Adler said, with a sigh. "To the layperson, and even to people in the know, what Green says is gibberish. He practically invented the ceti particles he discovered. It came from inside his drugged-up mind," Adler said, tapping the side of his head. "No publication has yet to print or even see a paper on this. And if they did, they would reject it offhand as the ravings of a mad scientist."

"And yet, you convinced us to believe him," Connelly said.

"Because it works, Rose. The boffins that built Reviver built it from Green's notes. Sure, it might have taken them the best part of six years to decipher those notes and twist them into a viable application, but we have a satellite in orbit, and it works."

"Back to Vernon," Connelly said. "How do you know it works?"

"I sent you the report on the puppy," Adler said.

"You sent a video of a scruffy dog covered in dirt," Ehle said. "It was dead."

"It was dead when Beane buried it in the ground, and, yes, it was dead again, shortly after he dug it up. But for about one minute, it was alive. Very much so." Adler turned to Bradley and said, "It works."

"Hey man," Bradley said. "I never said it didn't. I just don't see what the fuck you're going to do with a bunch of dead dogs on the battlefield – today or in fuck knows how many years into the future."

"Especially dead dogs that die a minute after they've been revived," Ehle said, drawing another smirk from Bradley.

"You're missing the point," Adler said. "You're glossing over the fact that Green's ceti particles do exactly what he said they would do. They are the big bang molecules we've been looking for. Green hit on a way to use them to revive dead cells. The combination of ceti and gamma radiation revives and regenerates life that once existed. And *that's* the key," he said, taking another look at each of the WARDEV representatives in the room. "As for the length of time the puppy lived, Vernon was a test run. We're ready with a second test over a wider area, at greater depth, with a much higher concentration of ceti particles." Adler took a breath, and said, "That's why I'm here, right?"

"Partly," Connelly said. "But carry on and we'll come to the second thing just as soon as you've finished."

"Okay," Adler said. He took a sip of coffee, buying time to think about *the second thing* before continuing with the details of test number two. "You've seen the brief for the second test."

"Seen it and approved it," Connelly said. "You know we have."

"Yes," Adler said. "But considering your concerns, I just wanted to know we were still on."

"Reviver has been approved, Glenn. Obviously. And given the amount of money that's been thrown at it already, it would be stupid, not to mention astronomically wasteful, not to continue. At the very least, we can always use it as an orbital weapon. The satellite photos of Vernon are sufficiently convincing to show us what a narrow beam blast of gamma radiation from orbit can do. I mean, you put tan lines on a patch of desert scrub, for God's sake. Think what that could do to a terrorist camp in another desert." Connelly turned to Bradley. "What do you say to that?"

"I'd say fuckin' A, ma'am," Bradley said. "Scorch the bastards without firing a shot, then send in a team to pick up the intel." Bradley laughed and said, "Just don't send the SEALs."

"Why not?" Connelly asked.

"Because it would be boring, ma'am. We're shooters. We need something to shoot. Any Joe can go in and sift through a bunch of irradiated bodies for intel." Bradley turned to Adler and said, "They might even find a few puppies."

"Thank you, Lieutenant," Connelly said. "If you'll give us the room."

"Yes, ma'am," Bradley said. He winked at Adler on his way out.

Connelly waited until he was gone, and the door was closed and sealed. "He has his uses, and there's no denying his skills on the ground. He's a leader. He hates, absolutely hates being a part of this, but we'll need him for Phase Two," she said.

"Yes, we will," Adler said. "And more like him."

"Training foreign paramilitaries is what he and his team are good at," Ehle said. "He won't fail us in that department. Although I think even Bradley might struggle to shape the teams you have in mind, Adler."

"We'll see."

"So, Libya?" Connelly said.

"Soon." Adler nodded and then reached for his coffee. "They're recalibrating Reviver as we speak."

"And ground ops? The perimeter?" Connelly turned to Ehle. "Should Bradley have been a part of that?"

"We're using Rhodium," Ehle said. "It's in progress and on schedule." She looked at Adler and said, "We'll be ready when you are."

"Well, I've taken care of the Libyans," Connelly said. "Or, rather, the Foreign Secretary has given them a certain incentive, and plenty of promises to encourage them to look the other way for an undefined period. Thankfully, your satellite," she said, looking at Adler, "is sufficiently accurate. We don't have to worry about collateral. At least, not above ground."

"That's correct," Adler said. "There will be some residual radiation from the gamma waves, but the simulation projections indicate it will remain beneath the sand and, provided no one walks across that area for a while, then…"

"Which is why we're using Rhodium," Ehle said before Adler could finish.

"Which brings us conveniently and uncomfortably to the second thing," Connelly said. She turned around to pick a small remote off the shelf beneath a flatscreen monitor mounted on the wall behind her. "This is helmet cam footage sent shortly after you arrived," she said. "Bradley hasn't seen it."

"Okay," Adler said. He took another sip of coffee as he stared at the grainy green and black images on the screen.

"I'll dim the lights," Ehle said. "It helps."

Adler barely noticed Ehle get up, and neither did he register the dimming of the light inside the SCIF. Adler's eyes were fixed on what looked like – if he even dared to believe it – a living, albeit barely breathing, dinosaur tucked between two large boulders in a desert landscape.

"This is just outside Vernon," Connelly said. "Your boy, Beane, sent it in. He had the presence of mind to collect all the videos and personal cameras from his team. His partner…"

"Claud," Adler said, barely a whisper.

"She handed out NDAs and appears to be sufficiently intimidating that all the men signed them. All of Beane's team, plus this woman here, who you might recognise, even with the helmet and night vision goggles."

"Is that Haines?"

"The one and only," Ehle said.

"Here's where it gets prickly," Connelly said. "There's some audio, and I'll play it in a second, but the upshot of it is your boy and your senator have some concerns. Yes, they are full of gushing awe over the results of the Vernon test. And, honestly, if I didn't worry about the media frenzy and world attention, a living dinosaur would shine on our not-so-little and soon to be very public secret, I might gush, too. But the fact is, even though your boy, Beane, handled this about as well as anyone can handle an unprecedented situation such as this. He's still got concerns – ethical, or moral? I don't give a shit. What concerns me is that the senator seems to share them too." Connelly paused the video on the image of Haines pointing at the dinosaur. "Apparently, it's a so-called Utahraptor. And if it hadn't been weakened by the radiation, and without the benefit of more ceti cells, it could have carried off more than..." She turned to Ehle and said, "What was the tally?"

"Two dogs, three chickens, and a cat. As far as we know."

"But thankfully no human casualties, apart from these two." Connelly clicked through the frames until the camera changed to Claud's camera with a closeup of Haines and Beane. "Green swan diving off the balcony I can live with. But you're going to have to deal with these two quietly, Glenn."

"Deal with them?" Adler shook his head. "I don't know what you're saying."

"Bullshit, Adler," Ehle said. "You know exactly what she's saying. If either of them sneezes in the wrong direction, you take them out of the game, permanently."

Connelly turned back to Adler and said, "And if you can't do it, I suggest the girl Claud does it. She seems to have a knack for getting things done."

"I can't ask Claud to kill Beane. He trusts her completely."

"Perfect," Connelly said. "Now, see that you fix this, Glenn." She pointed at the door and said, "We're done here."

Adler pushed back his chair. He took a moment as conflicting thoughts of liquidating Haines and Beane merged with the image of a dinosaur in his head.

Dead puppies were one thing, but a dinosaur, dead for over a million years, was another thing entirely.

It worked, he thought. *It really worked.*

10

Luci held her breath as the pilot of the *Afriqiyah Airways* Airbus A320 bumped the aircraft gently onto the runway at Misrata International Airport. Six years of war in Libya, part of the so-called Arab Winter, had ravaged the country and especially the coastal towns, but Sugar had assured Luci that, just three years later, although there were still plenty of problems to be overcome, there really was little to worry about.

"And the gang's going to look after you, honey. It's not a problem."

The gang met Luci in arrivals, and if she had been in doubt as to who she was supposed to meet, Jamillah Zaman put Luci at ease with the first hug as the thirty-two-year-old Libyan *fixer* fixed everything, expediting Luci's transition from the airport and into the red Toyota HiLux, complete with a roof rack overflowing with crates and cardboard boxes lashed to the bars, parked just outside the sand-coloured airport terminal.

"Fahd will take care of your bags," Jamillah said, brushing a curl of jet-black hair that escaped her hijab. "And then we'll just go. Okay?"

"Yes," Luci said as she blinked in the sunlight and suddenly felt weak in the heat.

"Water!" Jamillah snapped her fingers at a

man with skin three shades darker than her own, smoking with two more men of similar medium height and build, admiring a newer and far less battered Toyota. "Fahd?"

"I'm okay," Luci said.

"No. *Not* okay." Jamillah waved her hands at Luci's face as if just moving the hot air might make it easier for Luci to breathe. "*Fahd!*"

The man called Fahd finally seemed to take the hint and jogged across the parking lot, flicking his cigarette to one side before stopping a discrete distance from Luci. He dipped his head, with a lock of thick black hair falling across his brow, before flashing Luci a cheesy grin with perfect, if a little crooked, teeth.

"Hello," Fahd said. He dipped his head again, and then brushed the thin moustache he wore and frowned as if he had thought about something important but had just forgotten it.

"Fahd!" Jamillah said. "Water!"

"Water," Fahd said. "Of course."

"Really, I'm okay," Luci said. But when Fahd pressed a cold bottle of water into her hands, she drank it greedily, draining half the bottle and spilling more than a little on her t-shirt.

"Okay," Jamillah said. "We go."

And they went, just as soon as Fahd had stuffed Luci's kitbag and satchel into the back of the HiLux. Jamillah helped Luci onto the backseat, excusing the gear piled behind the driver's seat and the litter of wrappers and empty plastic bottles on the floor.

"Ready?" Fahd said as he climbed behind the

wheel.

"Go," Jamillah said.

Luci thought about asking about why they were in such a hurry, and then forgot all about it as Fahd started the engine and pumped the gas before accelerating out of the parking space and onto the Coastal Road, which, as Jamillah pointed out, wasn't very close to the coast at all.

"We take the Coastal Road, and then turn right onto Waddan-Abu Qurayn, following that deep, *deep*..." She raised her eyebrows as she looked at Luci. "Deep into the desert. And then sometime later, past the military base where you might have flown, if I had time to fix it, and then onto Waddan-Zillah. After which..." Jamillah stopped talking, and then fished another bottle of water from a cup holder in the dashboard. "Drink, Miss Luci, before you pass out. Okay?"

"Really, I'm..."

"Not okay," Jamillah said. She slapped Fahd on the arm as he turned to look at Luci, said something in Arabic, and then turned back to Luci. "You are like an English flower. So pale. Okay? You need to drink. We will drive. And maybe stop once in a while for food, or to pee, when we can." Jamillah leaned closer to Luci and said, "Do you need to pee? I never asked. It is a long journey. Okay?"

"I'm okay," Luci said. "I don't need to pee."

"Sleep then? Maybe you should sleep. The Americans slept all the way. You can sleep. Okay?"

"Jamillah," Fahd said. "The English is okay.

Okay?"

"Yes, *okaaaaaay*," Jamillah said. She gave Luci a last look and then turned to face forward. Jamillah fiddled with the radio until she found a song she liked and then, swaying in tune with the beat, she raised her hands and sang along. "Iman Aldresy," she said, turning to look at Luci. "You know him? You've heard him before, no?"

"No…" Luci said, but as Jamillah swayed and Fahd slowed for traffic, the gentle repetitive beat with instruments she simply couldn't define, completed the transportation from the chilly thunderbox at the end of her parents' English garden, to the desert of North Africa that so many English men and women had been drawn to. Luci suddenly understood the appeal, even if she had yet to understand why. Fahd shot her another cheesy grin, and a look that was neither suggestive nor discrete, as if he was entitled to look at her, but meant no harm by it, no offence. It was, Luci felt, at once strangely unnerving and yet somehow natural, with an ease that suggested it was okay to look at each other, and that looking, rather than pretending not to look but still *looking* as Westerners often did, made it easier to talk and to relax in each other's company, no matter how different the culture might be.

"It is your first time," Fahd said, more of a statement than a question. He looked at Luci again, and then drove forward when Jamillah slapped his arm and pointed at the gap between them and the next vehicle.

"In Libya?"

"The desert," Fahd said. "We are in the desert. Libya is an ocean in the sand."

"It can't be an *ocean*," Jamillah said. She turned to Luci and said, "Fahd is still learning English. Okay? He makes all kinds of mistakes. But you will learn him."

"I'll *teach* him?"

"No." Jamillah shook her head. "You will *learn* him. You'll find him out. Fahd is going to be your guide. Okay? In the desert." Jamillah pointed at her chest and said, "My name doesn't mean so much. But Fahd means *panther*. So he is a hunter. Okay?"

"Okay," Luci said. And then, "*Yes*."

"His last name, *Najjar*. It means… Er." Jamillah paused, searching for the word. "Yes. Okay. I have it. It means person who builds things… In wood."

"A carpenter?" Luci said.

"Yes. Okay. A carpenter. Exactly. So…" Jamillah grinned and said, "Fahd can hunt for things, and he can make things too. So, he's like a fixer, like me, just not so good with talking."

"I think his English is fine," Luci said, catching herself talking *about* Fahd, even though he was within arm's reach if she leaned forward. "I mean, it's fine, Fahd. It's good. I understand," she said. Then, looking at Jamillah, she added, "I understand you both. Much better than my Arabic."

"You speak Arabic?"

"No, Jamillah. I don't."

"Hey. No problem. We have twenty hours. We will teach you."

Luci sagged a little, wondering if she could remind Jamillah that she had suggested she sleep as much as possible, and how she might say that politely, without causing some cultural rift between them. She wondered this at the same time her body sweated, and her mouth dried, and the music slipped into her pores, until Jamillah snapped her fingers in front of Luci's face.

"I'm kidding," she said. "You have to drink. You have to sleep. And if you have to pee, you just say so. Fahd will stop. He will probably smoke. We can pee. And then we drive. Okay?"

"Yes," Luci said. "Yes, that's fine."

An absent thought passed through her mind as she wondered if this was how it was for Joci when she arrived somewhere hot, somewhere new, and then the thought was gone as Luci closed her eyes. She opened them again, forced a smile for Jamillah, and then closed her eyes once more as Fahd settled into a steady pace on a long straight road heading further and further south into the desert.

Luci stirred when the cooler breeze of the night drifted through the HiLux' windows. She blinked when Jamillah gently shook her awake, teasing her out of the vehicle to use a bathroom. Fahd filled the tank with gasoline from a jerry can he took from the roof. Jamillah followed Luci to the bathroom, pointing her at the toilet, making sure she was awake, and then promising good food as soon as she was finished.

Luci yawned as she stepped out of the square mud brick and palm trunk building, nodding when Jamillah asked if she was hungry, and again when she pressed a pastry into Luci's right hand.

The food was better than good.

Insistent spices exploding on Luci's tongue demanded her attention as she bit into what Jamillah called a *bureek*.

"Pastry, onion, beef, butter, and spices," she said. "It's good? Okay?"

"It's very good," Luci said.

Fahd leaned against the side of the HiLux, halfway through his own *bureek*. Luci looked around, amazed that she had missed the roadside brazier, like an opportunistic truck stop café in the middle of the desert. She tilted her head back. The sky was…

Luci swallowed.

She couldn't describe the sky.

Was it purple? Blue? Not quite black.

"Luci," Jamillah said. "You are okay?"

"I'm…" Luci bit her bottom lip as she smiled. "I'm *more than* okay. This is… amazing."

"It's special," Jamillah said. "Night in the desert is where we come from. Where people were born, you know?"

"I think so."

"Sure, there are many histories, and some say people came from here, and from there. But when you come to the desert – like you, for the first time – you know. You *know*?"

"Yes."

"And now you are here. I don't think you can

leave. It is a sickness." Jamillah shrugged. "I have seen it many times. Fahd has seen it too. People come here. They get sick. Some of them go home. Of course, they do. They take the sickness home with them, and it eats them. You know? A little every day. Little by little. But others, they are so sick, they can't imagine leaving." Jamillah reached out to brush Luci's hair from her cheek. She looked into Luci's brown eyes and nodded. "You have the sickness. I know it." Jamillah turned. "Fahd?"

"What?"

"Come here," she said.

Fahd finished his *bureek* and then pulled a soft rag from his pocket to wipe his fingers. "What is wrong?" he said.

"Luci is sick. You see it?"

Fahd took a moment to look at Luci, staring in that same unperturbed way that sent a subtle tremble through Luci's body that she had yet to define.

"Yes," Fahd said with a nod. "She's sick. And so soon."

"For some it goes quick," Jamillah said. "Not like the Americans. Not even the woman with the sweet name."

"Sugar," Luci said.

"Yes, sugar and sweet," Jamillah said. She pressed her finger to the side of her face, close to her eye, and said, "Sugar has a different look. She sees under the sand. She doesn't see the desert. She sees its histories. The men see heat. They see sand. They are uncomfortable. They are sick too –

sick for home. But not you. We have seen it. You are sick." Jamillah smiled. "It is good. Okay?"

"Yes," Luci said. "It is good."

"But," Jamillah said, pointing at the stars. "We must go. You can be sick as long as you want. But it is better to drive at night. Fahd will drive. We will sleep. Maybe stop and eat more *bureek*. But for now, we go. Okay?"

Luci nodded.

She didn't move.

"Come," Fahd said, waving for Jamillah to follow him. "She will meet us in the car."

"Be quick, Luci," Jamillah said.

"I will."

Luci let them walk on ahead, and then, tilting her head back, she stared up at the purple, blue, black sky, and the impossible number of stars that filled it. She thought of Joci, wondered if she was looking up at that same moment, and if she was sick, too?

"I get it, sis," Luci said. "Finally, I get it."

And then, with a single honk of the horn, Fahd reminded her it was time to go, and Luci walked across the sand to begin the next leg of her adventure.

PART
II

11

Last-minute visas, shots for something Jay had never heard of, followed by a reaction to the shots that put the old Warbird in bed for three days, delayed Jay's arrival in the desert. A military transport landing at Kufra Airport outside Al-Jawf picked up a little time, but not enough to stop Jay's team barraging him with as many variations on *take your time, old man* and *good job we were here to get things done* they could think of. While the team seemed genuinely pleased to have their leader on Libyan sand, Scruffette, Marion *Maid* Thompson's chocolate Labrador looked as miserable as Jay felt when the heat enveloped him, and he got the first taste of Libyan sand in his mouth as the wind blew across the apron. Gray *Jazzman* Charles, the real *old man* of the team – three years older than Jay's thirty-two years – took care of unloading the additional gear from Jay's flight. A small squad of Rhodium personnel helped the tall black man. Jay didn't recognise any of them, and half of them looked local.

"Sparrow?" Jay said, nodding at Josh Wheeler, the youngest helicopter pilot Jay had yet to greet. "Sitrep?"

"The situation, boss?" Sparrow, a thin white

man who earned his call sign from his spindly frame more than his ability to fly, shrugged. He ran his hand through his red hair as the wind grazed the team's skin with more sand and said, "The situation is I don't have a bird."

"No helicopter?"

"Nope." Sparrow tucked his hands inside his tactical vest, providing ample opportunity for any member of the team to tell him he *had* wings, if they chose to mention the young pilot's knobbly elbows sticking out at right angles to his body, but it was just too damned hot to bother. "But the good news is the first perimeter fence is up."

"It's a *wall*," Marion said as she pulled a tattered ball cap firmly onto her shaved head. She tugged a foldable bowl out of her vest, crouched beside Scruffette, filled the bowl with water and encouraged the three-year-old dog to drink while she talked. "It's impressive, actually. It's about sixty feet high, with substantial guard posts in the compass corners, and a lookout tower every quarter mile."

"Every quarter mile?" Jay said. "Just how big is this area?"

"They didn't tell you?" Sparrow lifted his head to the thin blue sky and muttered, "Oh, man…"

"Boss," Marion said. "It's fifty square miles. They've been building this for months, I tell you. There's one section we need to lock off in the southeast corner, but they're already working on the second wall – perimeter two."

"And they're nearly finished, too," Sparrow

said. "Apart from…"

"The southeast corner?" Jay reached out for the water bottle in Marion's hand, nodding his thanks when she handed it to him. "So, we've got two perimeters. Made of what?"

"It's Hesco Bastion mesh units packed with sand," Marion said.

Sparrow laughed, adding, "Plenty of that around here, boss."

"Go on, Maid," Jay said with a nod to Marion.

"It's just like Afghanistan, scaled up, obviously, with three units stacked on top of each other. Each unit is a little shy of fifteen feet. The corner guard posts sit on a square pillar four units deep. The observation platform on top of the roof gives you another six feet," Marion said. "Observation posts between them are a little lower, but then there's fuck all to see, boss."

"Got it," Jay said, taking another swallow of water. "Gates?"

"Two main ones close to each other. One in the west wall, close to the southern corner, and a second, slightly smaller, about halfway along the southern wall. Base camp is built around the western gate."

"You're laughing," Jay said. "What am I missing?"

"This whole thing, boss," Marion said, her blue eyes flashing in the sun. "It's all backwards. We're used to the camp being *inside* the perimeter. Apart from small sangars with sandbags and a tin roof in each corner of the camp…" Marion paused. "If we were attacked, from *outside* the perimeter." She shook her head. "We'd last maybe a few minutes before we got steamrolled into the desert." She looked at Jay and said, "If you know something we don't, then we need to hear it, boss."

"Rhodium built a prison in the desert," Jazzman said as he wandered over to join them. "And we've been demoted to prison guards. Ain't that right, boss?" he said, looking at Jay.

"More or less," Jay said. "Although there's not much more I can tell you. And I think I know less than you."

"We'll catch you up on the drive in," Jazzman said. He jerked a thumb at the Humvee military vehicle parked in front of the Oshkosh MTVR supply truck, giving Sparrow and Marion their cue to *mount up*. The remaining Rhodium personnel divided themselves between the truck and a second Humvee behind it. Jazzman waited until the others had gone before gripping Jay's hand and pulling him into a tight bear hug. "It's good to see you, brother," he said.

"You too," Jay said. He raised his voice to compete with the roar of an incoming flight. "You look worried. What's up?"

"Seeing you in the desert is enough to make anyone worry. You said, and I quote, *no more fucking sand*."

"I did say that," Jay said. "But that's not what's worrying you, is it?"

Jazzman pulled off his wide-brimmed Boonie hat and ran his hand over his smooth scalp. "Like

I said, Rhodium has built a prison in the desert," he said. "And someone threw a shit-tonne of money at it to get it built quickly. But there's nothing there, Jay. It's just desert. Nothing inside the wire, apart from a couple of small camps from the expeditionary teams who came here to scout the place. At least, that's what I guess they were doing. We met them on the way out, but they left a tonne of gear in those camps, like caches."

"Yeah," Jay said. "That part I *was* briefed on."

"So it's not a prison, right?" Jazzman snorted in the heat. "I mean, you don't leave caches of gear, food, and water on the inside of a prison. Unless, of course, this is some kind of weird shit reality game, where we let a whole load of celebrity wannabes run loose inside the perimeter in some crazy TV contest. Because, if that's what this is…" Jazzman shook his head. "I didn't sign up for that, Jay. Neither did they." He pointed at Sparrow and Marion beside the Humvee. "And neither did you."

"I didn't," Jay said. "But I don't think you have to worry about some *Battle Royale* last person standing reality show. I don't think even Rhodium would stoop that low."

"No?" Jazzman prodded Jay in the chest. "Look who they put in charge."

"Harsh," Jay said, as his old friend laughed.

"You pay me to be blunt, brother."

"No, I pay you to watch my six. And," Jay said with a nod to the rest of the team. "To watch theirs as well."

"I've got you covered," Jazzman said. "You know it." He tugged a bottle of water from his vest and took a long swallow. Jazzman waited for the newly arrived passenger plane to power down before continuing. "Which brings me to the other thing."

"What's that?"

"The hardware we just unpacked. That's some serious inventory."

"Small arms?"

"A few," Jazzman said. "And that's the point. We've got grenade launchers – all kinds. There's a whole crate of Barrett M82 50 calibre rifles. M2 Browning 50 calibre machine guns in the towers. Shit, Jay, there's even 50 cal Desert Eagle handguns. Apart from a bunch of M4s, there's not much that isn't 50 cal or up." Jazzman laughed. "We can blow shit up and punch holes through the sides of shit, but there's nothing with finesse, apart from maybe the Barretts. If this *is* a prison, I have no clue who the hell they're going to put inside it. But unless carnage is on the menu, this isn't the typical ordnance I would expect for guard duty. This is *heavy* duty."

"Yeah, I see where you're going…"

"Shit," Jazzman said, cutting him off. "I forgot all about the miniguns mounted to the dodgems."

"The *what*?"

"There's a bunch of two-seater vehicles with bubble canopies and crazy weapons mounted on each side. They're armed but not armoured. Fast and fun, they pack a punch, but you don't want anyone shooting back at you."

"So, we've got a lot of stuff, just *weird* stuff. Is that what you're saying?"

"I guess it is."

"Okay, well, let's worry about it once we get to camp. I am dog tired, and the heat isn't helping."

"Understood," Jazzman said. "Let's get you home."

Jazzman gave the signal to leave and then walked Jay to the Humvee. Jay waved Sparrow into the front seat and settled in the back, with Marion and Scruffette panting between them.

"She's hot," Marion said. "We all are."

"Yeah," Jay said. "It's the fucking desert!"

Scruffette flopped in front of the air-conditioning unit in what had to be the best team room Jay had seen in any combat deployment. An L-shaped couch faced a robust flatscreen TV that doubled as a screen for briefings and entertainment. The Hesco walls blocked all natural light, and LED tubes were strung between them together with the coloured Christmas lights Sparrow always managed to sneak into every team room they had occupied. The lack of a helicopter gave the pilot plenty of time for interior decoration and the team left him to it. Two fold-up cots tucked end to end behind tables for ruggedized computers, and another for maps and planning completed the setup, with a small space for beverages – hot and cold – in the corner furthest from the door. The camp kitchen, staffed by a mix of Rhodium and local personnel, was inside the small compound outside the team room. Sleeping areas were gathered under cloth awnings tied to the Hesco walls.

After a surprisingly good meal supplemented with local savoury pastries Jazzman had discovered in the week prior to Jay's arrival, the reluctant Rhodium employee was almost ready to change his mind about being back in the desert. He took a moment to tour the small camp with Sparrow, noting how few they were…

"About thirty, including you, boss," Sparrow said.

… and how many Jay thought he needed to patrol the fifty square miles of wall.

"Another twenty would do it." Sparrow shrugged, adding, "If we had a chopper…"

"We don't," Jay said. "Not yet."

"We might?"

"I'll make it my top priority."

Sparrow gave Jay his usual wish list on the walk back to the team room. Jay nodded and tutted at the mention of various extraneous items he doubted Rhodium would agree to. Although a quick glance around the camp suggested Rhodium was digging deeper into their pockets than ever before, which, naturally, only made Jay nervous.

"I'll tell you straight," he said, once the rest of the team, including Scruffette, was seated comfortably on the couch in front of him. "This one doesn't feel quite right."

Marion and Sparrow nodded. Jazzman simply looked at Jay. Scruffette snored softly in the breeze of the air-conditioning unit.

"Malcolm," Jay said.

"Fucking *Malcolm.*" Sparrow rolled his eyes and then apologised, waving for Jay to continue.

"Fucking Malcolm told me as much as he could," Jay said. "Obviously, that was next to nothing, considering the scale of the area we're supposed to guard." Jay paused to sigh. "Honestly, I don't know what we're doing here, and I don't think Malcolm, or even Rhodium, knows much more than we do. But we're here. On the ground. In a poorly defended camp in the middle of the desert." Jay pointed at the maps pinned to boards hung from the Hesco walls. "You've already done the groundwork." Jay nodded at Jazzman, knowing he would be the one to gather all the intel necessary for them to do their job. "Now I want to take a good look inside, before they close the perimeter. My guess is things will happen quickly after that."

"I hope so," Jazzman said. "Otherwise, we're guarding a big chunk of nothing for no reason."

"There'll be a reason," Jay said. "I'm just not entirely sure we're going to like it." He started to say more, only to stop when something marked on the map closest to him caught his eye. "And what's that?" He took a step closer to study the map. "Is that a local village or…"

"Here we go," Marion said with a sigh. Scruffette stirred in her lap as she leaned forward to look at Jazzman. "Are you going to tell him?"

"Yeah," Jazzman said as he pushed himself off the couch. "That," he said, jabbing the map with a thick finger as he stood beside Jay, "is your first headache."

"Mine?"

"Yours," Jazzman said with a nod of his head. "We've tried. We even had the local chief – or something – try. But the woman there…"

"What woman?"

"Sugar Albuquerque," Marion said. "From Cal State. She's on a dig, for bones and shit."

"Fossilised shit," Sparrow said.

"Yeah, anyway." Jazzman tapped the map. "They've got a little camp with three Americans, a couple of indigenous people…"

"He means *Libyans*," Marion said.

"And one English rose," Jazzman said with another slow nod. "In the middle of the desert, right where our wall is going."

"The southeast corner," Jay said, tracing the perimeter of the unfinished wall on the map.

"Unfinished," Marion said.

"Problematic," Jazzman said.

Sparrow smiled and said, "Fun."

Scruffette snored, and Jay cursed.

"I hate the desert," he said.

12

Luci spent the first day at the dig in a haze, acclimatising to the heat and the routine of Sugar Albuquerque's camp. Sugar took the young PhD under her wing in the shape of a faded purple and much patched umbrella, something she said she picked up from the English. With her hand nestled in the crook of the older woman's arm, Luci was reminded of Joci and wondered what her sister would make of the sight of the self-confessed but spry *fossil* leading Joci's younger and heat-weary sister across narrow planks above deep ditches straight out of an *Indiana Jones* movie, beneath canvas awnings erected to protect trestle tables littered with finds from the dig, and to and from the water containers when Sugar insisted Luci hydrate with another half-litre of water.

"You're no good to me lying on your cot, honey," Sugar said.

It was a familiar refrain, offered on days two, three, and four during the week of orientation Sugar had planned for Luci. The afternoon of day five was no different, as Sugar made sure Luci filled her water bottle before leading her back to the trestle tables to escape the afternoon heat. "Now, drink up… That's it. Finish the bottle. And come over here."

Luci drained the bottle and then followed Sugar to where she stood in the middle of two trestle tables. Fahd lounged under a tarp draped from the Toyota as he waited to unload the weekly supply truck Jamillah promised was én route, but had yet to appear. Jamillah napped inside one of three tents that made Luci think of the Bedouin of the Sahara or, more likely, the Berbers of Libya. Sugar's two male assistants, Trevor Evans and Jeremy Watts, slept in the tent beside Jamillah's. But despite the heat, Sugar confessed that *naptime*, as she called it, was her favourite time of day.

"Because everyone else is asleep," she said with a conspiratorial wink at Luci. "Now…" Sugar gestured at the table on her left with a wave of a sun-wrinkled hand. "Tell me what you see."

Luci nodded and took a step closer to the table. She lifted her head, glancing once in Fahd's direction, before biting her lip to hide the flutter of something she still needed to process inside. Luci did her best to stifle a smile. Fahd lifted his head, just enough for Luci to see his eyes, before a soft tut followed by the word *focus* directed Luci's attention back to the table.

"This is a small ornithischian," Luci said as she picked up the fossil of a small bird-like claw. "There are five fingers," she said, tracing them with the tip of a soft brush from the table.

"Good," Sugar said. "Keep going. Tell me more."

"Ornithischians have hip bones, like birds,

hence the name."

"And?"

Luci turned to look at Sugar and smiled as the desert light twinkled in the expedition leader's eyes. Sugar's long grey hair, tied in a loose bun, was coated with dust and sprinkled with sand, just like Luci's rough bob. Both women wore a sheen of sweat and silica on the exposed parts of their skin, and Luci's hands were already turning a light brown, almost as dark as Sugar's, but not nearly as dark as…

"Focus," Sugar said as Luci's eyes drifted. "You might be the youngest PhD I've had the pleasure of dragging into the field, but I need your, head not your hormones. *Focus*, honey. Fahd isn't going anywhere."

"Fahd?"

Sugar tilted her head to one side and gave Luci *the look*.

"Right," Luci said. "Focus."

She *focused*, dialling in to the fossil in her hand, pushing the adventure of arriving in Africa and driving into the desert into the back of her mind as she thought about the reason she was in the field at all. Her supervisors and peers expected Luci to continue with post-doctoral work, but encouraged her to build her academic portfolio with more field experience. Strings were pulled, introductions were made, and Luci joined Sugar's team.

"And now I have to earn it," she whispered.

"What's that, honey?" Sugar said. "Could have been the wind. I'm sure you said…"

"Lesothosaurus," Luci said. "Probably. But if it was found here, then it's further north than the area in which it was found."

"That being?"

"Lesotho," Luci said with a smile. "Easy one."

"Go on," Sugar said.

"Lesothosaurus is from the Jurassic, about 200 million years ago. We think it was about this high," Luci said, bending to place a flat palm beside her knee. "Maybe a little higher, but not by much," she said. "It was roughly a three feet long. We know it travelled in family groups. It may or may not have lived in burrows."

"And the claws?"

"Fingers," Luci said. "Five on each hand. That and the size is what gave it away. The fingers were probably not that good at grasping."

"And how do you know that?"

"I don't." Luci shrugged. "But that's what I read. To really know it, then I would have to study it closely."

"As you are doing right now," Sugar said.

"Then this *is* from the dig site."

"Yes." Sugar frowned as she saw a trail of dust in the distance. "Although not *this* site. There is another, smaller dig a few miles north of here, deeper in the desert. It's a partial dig begun by a good friend at from the geology department at the University of Tripoli. Only…" She sighed as the dust trail grew in size, suggesting there was more than one vehicle on the way to the camp. "He was moved on by the military."

"The Libyan Army?" Luci said.

"Possibly, although it's hard to tell. It could have been a government backed militia." Sugar reached for Luci's hand and clutched it. "Now, listen to me, before I convince myself not to ask this of you."

"Ask me what?"

"Those strings your peers pulled… Well, honey, hate to break it to you, but they didn't work. Your application was tossed into the slush pile, leaving me with a whole bunch of Trevors and Jeremys. Don't get me wrong, they are fine young men." Sugar rolled her eyes, adding, "Young*ish*. But they are cardboard cut-outs of the last thousand or so applicants I have seen. But you…" Sugar squeezed Luci's hand. "You look just like another English girl I read about in a magazine. I thought you might even be her. You're so alike."

"You're talking about Joci," Luci said.

"Am I?"

"My sister, the adventurer."

"Well, yes. I don't remember her name – I have a better head for longasuarus names, but there was a grainy image of this girl with your face. And when I chanced upon your photo attached to a sheaf of paper in the slush pile, well… I have to admit, I saw an opportunity."

"So you wanted my sister?" Luci swallowed, suddenly in need of more water. "Not me?"

"Dear girl, Luci. *Honey*. I wanted you. The PhD who can identify a Lesothosaurus after handling a cast of its five fingers in her hand for less than three minutes – *including* the extra time spent on our friend Fahd resting in the sun over there." Sugar patted Luci's hand and then let go as the young PhD added another rush of colour to her sunburned cheeks. "My Trevors and Jeremys tried to convince me it was Archaeopteryx…"

"About 150 million years ago," Luci said. "Found in Germany."

"Yes," Sugar said.

"Archaeopteryx was carnivorous and half the size of Lesothosaurus. And Lesothosaurus was a herbivore."

"Now you're just being cute," Sugar said. "And I like that. But what I *need* is for you to disappear."

"You want me to what?"

"You see those dust trails?" Sugar pointed and Luci turned to look. "That is bad news coming our way. I'm sure there are Americans among them. My friend in Tripoli mentioned foreign hands pulling strings to yank him out of the desert. But to the north…" Sugar tapped the cast in Luci's hand. "My friend, Mazin," she said, with another surge of desert light in her eyes. "He says he has uncovered one whole and a partial, but a sandstorm covered his dig site, and before he could uncover them again, the military removed him. There is also a cave." Sugar took a breath and then cursed as the two approaching vehicles drew close enough to reveal the antennae and weapons that identified them as military vehicles. "Say nothing when they come. Let me do the talking," Sugar said. "In fact. You could even hide."

"Hide?"

"Yes. You must hide, honey." Sugar waved to Fahd, then called out to him to hurry. "It's a big ask," she said, as Fahd walked towards them. "But I think this is a big find. It would mean so much to me, and to Mazin, if someone with the same skills and dedication that you have shown would finish his work…"

"Sugar…"

"And document it. Drive in, and drive out," she said, reaching for Fahd's hand as he ducked under the edge of the tent. "Fahd will take you. He knows the way, and he knows the desert. He will protect you with his life. I know it." Sugar turned to Fahd and said, "You will, won't you?"

"I will," Fahd said with a slight crease of his brow. "What do you want me to do?"

"Take Luci north, to the burrows and caves."

"Mr Mazin's caves?"

"Yes, the very ones." Sugar nodded. "Take Luci there. Help her. And then bring her to Tripoli with the evidence." She turned back to Luci and said, "A find like this will put Africa firmly on the map again. It will bring resources to Libya – much needed resources. So much has been neglected during the war, *after* the war. Money is prioritised, and what money there is always, *always* comes with a rider, demanding this or that. The World Bank *helps* countries like Libya to repay their debt through privatization of public services and the plundering of natural resources. A flock of Lesothosaurus in a cave in the desert in Libya means nothing to them. But to us…" She pressed her hand to her heart and then to Luci's. "It is what we live and breathe for. To Mazin…" She shook her head as if the enormity of what it meant to her friend was too much to grasp. "It will save his department, save his job. It will put food on his family's table. And I mean exactly that, honey."

"Yes…" Luci said. She turned as the military vehicles – a large Humvee she recognised from a movie she had once seen, and a smaller bubble-like car, a third of the Humvee's size – skidded to a stop in a cloud of dust in front of the tents. "But I don't…"

"You don't have to agree this second, but…" Sugar bobbed her head from one side to the other and said, "Maybe if you thought about it for the next thirty minutes?"

"Sugar, I…"

"Talk to Fahd," Sugar said, taking the Libyan's hand and pressing it into Luci's. "He knows Mazin. He will convince you." Sugar grabbed her umbrella and, holding it like a sword, she marched out of the tent towards two American-looking men as they climbed out of the Humvee. "Hey!" she said, pointing the tip of the umbrella at the man in full military gear and sporting a dusty chin curtain beard around his jaw. "This is *my* camp. You're out of your jurisdiction, Soldier!"

"Fahd," Luci said. She shook her head a little, as if trying to make sense of what Sugar had just said, what she was asking her to do. And then she looked down, pulling her fingers sharply out of Fahd's hand, as another bout of colour burned her cheeks. "I don't know…"

"It's all right," Fahd said. "*I* know. Sugar told me what she needed. Mazin needs it. I think, maybe… *maybe* you need it too."

Luci turned her head as the soldier raised his voice to compete with Sugar, revealing an American accent – different, but just as strong as the expedition leader's. She looked at the cast in her hand and then closed her eyes, wondering if Sugar's story was real. And, if it was, was she, twenty-six-year-old Lucille Hampton, identical but *younger* twin of up-and-coming adventurer Jocelyn Hampton, about to follow in her sister's footsteps on an adventure in search of treasure?

"Yes," she breathed. "I think I am."

"Luci?" Fahd dipped his head to catch her eye. "You have made a decision?"

She nodded.

"Good," he said, flashing that same perfectly crooked smile Luci knew was partly responsible for that strange flutter in her body and the dry tongue in her mouth. "Then come with me. Everything is ready."

"It's ready?"

Fahd nodded at the red Toyota parked to one side of the military vehicles.

"Sugar told me to pack on your very first day," he said. "She knew you would say yes."

"Okay," Luci said, with a smile, as she borrowed one of Jamillah's favourite words. "Then I guess I am ready."

"When they go, we go," Fahd said, and Luci agreed.

13

Jay stewed on the drive back to the Rhodium camp, with a glance over his shoulder between curses until the Cal State dig, tents, and that *damned professor* were hidden behind a wall of dust behind the Humvee and a single dodgem. Jazzman drove without a word, waiting for Jay to speak first, knowing from past experience that his team leader would need a moment, and then a moment more, before he was ready.

"Why is it?" Jay said, with another fruitless glance over his shoulder. "We never have problems with the indigenous folk. You tell them to move, and they just move."

"Probably because of all the guns, boss," Jazzman said with a shrug. He grinned, hoping to lighten the mood as he added, "It's just a theory."

"Right..." Jay scratched at a crust of sand and dirt in his beard. "You said there was a Libyan dig?"

"Further to the north." Jazzman nodded. He raised his voice over the throaty growl of the Humvee's engine as he accelerated up a shallow but soft dune that had drifted across the road. "They downed tools and left without so much as a raised eyebrow. But then we did have a Libyan official with us. He said something, and I swear the Libyans at the dig site trembled. God knows what he threatened them with, but it worked."

"And here we are, with some damned professor from our own country claiming she has a right to be where she is, that…" Jay clenched his fist as he took a breath. "I don't know," he said after a long pause. "I'm tired of this. I was tired of it before Malcolm forced me to take this gig." He took one last look over his shoulder and swore. "Now I guess I'm just tired *and* pissed about it."

"Boss?"

"I mean, look at this," Jay said, gesturing at the Hesco wall and the engineers and their diggers from the private contractors churning up more dust as they packed the mesh frames with sand, racing to finish the wall according to a schedule that was still unconfirmed but *tight*, as Jazzman put it when he commented on the activity around the base. "What the hell are we even doing here?"

"Boss," Jazzman said, trying for a second time to disrupt Jay's negative cycle. "You'll find out in the briefing this afternoon. But before then…"

"Don't say it," Jay said with a shake of his head.

"I'm *gonna* say it, boss." Jazzman pointed at the camp clustered around the gates as they approached. He started to speak, but Jay beat him to it.

"We're totally exposed," Jay said. "No camp security whatsoever."

"The guns are facing into the desert, boss.

But," Jazzman said, picking up where he left off, "if you promise to get a few hours on your cot, I'll work up a camp defence detail."

"I should have done it the minute I arrived."

"Sure, you could have, but then the focus is on what's *inside* the wire. Or whatever the hell they're going to put inside it. Hell, boss, this could be some billionaire's wet dream we're guarding. Maybe he wants to hunt elephants or some shit, and they're flying them in just as soon as the perimeter is up."

"Could be a *she*," Jay said.

"Who? The billionaire?"

"Why not?"

"Sure, boss." Jazzman slowed as they approached the camp, letting the dust cloud settle behind them over the last quarter mile instead of dragging it with them to fill the tents, shoes, and food when they made an abrupt stop. "But I've never heard of a female billionaire. I'm not saying they don't exist, but you never hear about them."

"Which might be the whole point," Jay said. He dipped his head to look up at the top of the Hesco wall, noting the smaller guard posts on either side of the gate – one man with a .50 cal. machine gun in each – and the top of the gate doors between them. "Should we have a sluice, or a funnel of some sort?"

"What?" Jazzman turned his head to look in the same direction. "You think this is some kind of refugee area? Maybe even a pandemic, something or other?"

"I have no idea," Jay said. "But you can get a

hell of a lot of tents inside fifty square miles." He swore and said, "We're going to read about this in the *Post* or the *Times*, I guarantee it."

"Yeah, well, I only read the sports pages, so I guess I'm fine, eh?"

Jay laughed. "You always were the smart one."

Jazzman looked at the younger man and laughed. "You think I'm smart? That's nice, boss." He slowed to a stop, parking between two more Humvees in a line of vehicles with three heavily armed dodgems at the far end. "I just don't let it get to me." He opened the door and said, "That's why they pay you the big bucks."

"Maybe if they did…"

"You'd still twist yourself up about it." Jazzman reached into the Humvee for his M4 carbine, slung it over one shoulder, and then pointed at the team sleeping quarters. "I'll wake you in two hours. That'll give you time for some of Maid's apocalyptically strong coffee before the briefing. All right?"

"Sure," Jay said with a nod. "Two hours."

Jazzman pointed at the sangars at each corner of the camp. "And I'll get some guys set up in the corners. You won't recognise the place when you wake up, boss, I promise."

Jay laughed, grabbed his M4 and climbed out of the Humvee. He waved at Jazzman on the way to his cot, and then slid onto it with his carbine cradled across his chest. Some of the less experienced Rhodium personnel called it overkill. Others thought it was a sign of trauma, but Jay and his team knew it was just good practice to sleep within reach of one's personal weapon. For the old Warbird, getting his head down in a poorly defended camp in the middle of the desert in a foreign country on a secret and undefined mission, it was simply common sense.

"Fucking desert," he said with a sigh as he closed his eyes.

The briefing was restricted to Jay's team and two engineers – one local, and a slight but well-built German who glanced at her watch every other minute as if she, if no one else, was on the clock. Jay's team made room for her and Jay on the L-shaped couch, but neither Jay nor Ulli Faber were ready to sit. The panoramic lens of the webcam captured them where they stood on either side of the couch.

"Popcorn time," Sparrow said as he squeezed into a spot between the local engineer and Jazzman. Scruffette lay sprawled over Marion's lap at the other end with her eyes fixed on Jay. Sparrow pointed at the timer displayed on the screen, counting down to connection, and said, "Let's go, Rhodium. I'm ready!"

The timer continued, then stopped at zero.

"Perfect," Jay whispered.

"We could always put a movie on," Sparrow said. "*Titanic* or…"

"*Titanic* in a desert?"

"Sure," Sparrow said, turning to Marion. "It makes sense. Think about it…"

"Think about it later," Jay said with a nod at

the screen as it flickered into life.

A hush fell around the team room as a trim man in his sixties with grey hair and a grey beard that almost hid the scar on his top lip waved at the camera.

"My name is Glenn Adler," he said. "And I'm the reason you're sitting where you are today." He paused for a few theatrical beats before adding, "Welcome to the Reviver Project."

"*Reviver*?" Sparrow looked from side to side. "Is that what he said?"

"Knock it off, Sparrow," Jay said. He turned to look at the screen. "Mr Adler?"

"Ah, Mr Styles, I presume," Adler said, turning to look at Jay. "You arrived safely, I trust?"

"I was delayed…" Jay shrugged. "I'm here now."

"And no doubt eager to know what you're doing guarding fifty square miles of sand in the desert?"

"Something like that, sir."

"Then let me begin," Adler said. He reached for a remote and then clicked a button to project a shared screen onto the flatscreen in the team room. "This is a satellite image of the area of operations. We've been monitoring your progress, Ms Faber." Adler turned within the small screen inserted in the top left-hand side of the map. "You've achieved a lot in a very short period of time…"

"It has been difficult," Faber said. She puffed at a lock of brown hair that escaped the baseball cap she wore and then glanced at her watch. "Tight. Very tight."

"And we are grateful." Adler nodded. "And perimeter number two?"

"On schedule," Faber said. "We will close the gap in perimeters one *and* two at the same time." She nodded at Jay. "There has been a delay."

"Right," Jay said. "That's on me, I guess." He returned Faber's nod before addressing Adler. "There's a small American team of archaeologists in the southeast corner of the project area. We expect them to move out by end of day."

"You expect it?"

"We ordered them to leave, Mr Adler. They weren't too pleased about it, but I'll send a couple of dodgems tonight to make sure they're gone."

"Dodgems?"

"And that's on me, Mr Adler, sir," Jazzman said, raising his hand. "It's the name I gave to some of the toys you sent us."

"And do you like your toys, Mr Charles?"

"Yes, sir." Jazzman grinned. "Very much so. Even if…"

"Yes?"

"Well, they're a little on the heavy side, sir. If you know what I mean?"

"By design, Mr Charles."

"And why is that?" Jay took a step forward. "Why the .50 cal? The grenade launchers…"

"And the personal Gruber 12 machine pistols, Mr Styles."

"The *what*?"

"Sent two days ago. Personal weapons for all of your team. You should have them tonight."

"The Gruber is another serious piece of kit, Mr Adler," Jay said. "But you haven't told us what we need it all for."

"Look at the map, Mr Styles," Adler said.

Jay and his team watched as the satellite image changed to a flat projection of the desert, the perimeter walls – finished for the purpose of the simulation – and a green cone that beamed down upon an area inside the second perimeter.

"*Reviver* is a delivery platform. Your team has been selected to guard the test area assigned to *Reviver*. Forty-eight hours from now, a satellite will irradiate the marked area with ceti particles…"

"With *what-the-fuck*?" Jazzman said. "If you'll excuse me, sir."

"You're excused," Adler said with a nod of his head and a smile that lingered while he talked, as if the *Reviver Project* was close to his heart and the older man was genuinely excited to share the details with Jay and his team. Adler's enthusiasm rubbed off on almost everyone in the team room, reducing the level of scepticism to a couple of concerned glances between Jay and the German engineer. "The ground will be *hot*, and should be avoided for another forty-eight hours."

"What kind of *hot*?" Jay said. "Like radioactive *hot*?"

"Yes, but nothing to worry about. Ceti particles have an incredibly short life. They tend to burn themselves out once they have been deployed."

"And what happens after deployment?" Jay swapped another glance with Faber. "What can we expect?"

"We don't know," Adler said.

"You don't know?"

"Mr Styles," Adler said. "I appreciate your concerns. But let me assure you and your team, you are not about to be subjected to harmful radiation. *Reviver* has been tested rigorously in the lab and in the field."

"And which poor nation did you blast in your test?" Jay said as he crossed his arms over his chest.

"Utah, actually," Adler said.

"No shit?" Sparrow said. He leaned forward. "You tested this shit in the States?"

"Correct, Mr Wheeler. Utah was the area chosen for a modest delivery of the ceti particles. The area you are guarding is considerably larger, of course."

"And did you have a perimeter around the test area in Utah?"

"No, Mr Styles. We did not. It was a small-scale test, with the depth of penetration limited to twelve inches." Adler paused. "We're going to go much deeper in the desert."

"And why do you need us, and all the guns, Mr Adler?" Jay gestured at his team.

Adler swapped the remote for a cup of coffee from the desk behind him and took a sip. "Simply put, Mr Styles, *Reviver* does exactly what it says on the tin – to coin a phrase. It *revives* things."

"Dead things?"

"Buried beneath the surface." Adler nodded. "Yes."

"I knew it," Sparrow said. "We're on zombie watch!"

"Wind your neck in, Sparrow," Jazzman said with a slap of the younger man's arm. He pointed at the screen, encouraging the pilot to listen.

"*Reviver* has some specific *dead things* – as you put it – that are of interest to the project." He looked at Jay and said, "I'm sending you a data packet, for your eyes only, Mr Styles." Adler turned back to the rest of the team. "It's just possible the test will be a bust, and beyond a few desert rats and the odd camel, *Reviver* might reveal nothing of interest."

Marion held up her hand. "You're saying these ceti particles can bring the dead back to life? I mean, you're *actually* saying that?"

"Yes."

"So the hardware we have…" Jazzman shook his head as if he wasn't quite ready to accept what he was about to say. "It's for big things?"

"Potentially," Adler said.

"Like…" Jazzman laughed. "Like *dinosaurs*?"

Jay waited for the team to settle, but kept a close eye on Faber as she cast a worried look in his direction.

"The walls, Mr Adler," she said.

"Will suffice," Adler said.

Jay stepped to one side, out of the camera's view. He drummed his fingers on his thighs, and then turned, heading for the door.

"Ah, Mr Styles?" Adler said.

Jay stopped.

"You can expect my packet momentarily."

Jay waved and stepped out of the team room.

"The fucking desert... with fucking *dinosaurs*." He took a breath and surveyed the camp, wondering how Malcolm had talked him into the mission, and then thinking of his mother, the health benefits. "And California."

Jay closed his eyes and tried to imagine long stretches of the Californian coast he remembered visiting once, in what seemed like a very long time ago. There was solace there, he knew, and if he just got through what had to be a *billionaire's wet dream*, as Jazzman had put it, then he might live long enough to enjoy it.

A long blast of a car horn disturbed his reverie and Jay opened his eyes as Sugar Albuquerque and her team surged past in a small convoy, windows down as they gave Jay the finger, and a mouthful of dust and sand as the archaeologist's furious wake blew into the Rhodium camp.

14

They travelled by night. Fahd kept the headlights switched off, but his smile – the same crooked smile Luci hoped to see each time she looked at him – was lit by the stars in that same velvet night sky Luci had struggled to describe only a week earlier when she first entered the desert of Libya.

Velvet.

It had taken longer than she might have expected to discover the word she wanted to describe the night, but as it sank over the dunes and vast expanses of sand, drawing cool air from the heavens to the parched land beneath the stars, Luci embraced it, and longed to be enveloped by it. Never before had she felt the peace of dark, open places as she did in the desert. There was an ancient magic here, greater than the so-called superpowers flexing their muscles across borders, or in spitting matches in contested areas. The magic, the kind that transcended time, resisted the ravages of the unrest – the *war* – in Libya, and Luci listened as Fahd talked of his family as they drove north, bumping and bouncing along a starlit trail, deeper into the desert.

"My sister was fighting," he said. "She was two years younger than me. I was ashamed that she was the first to take up arms, to join the struggle."

"For whom?" Luci said. "Which side?"

"Does it matter?" Fahd looked at Luci, then dismissed the question with a wave of his hand. "It mattered, once, perhaps. But so much death. There was destruction. So much. It did not matter. How could it matter? It just had to stop." He looked at Luci again. "It had to stop," he said. "I made it so."

"You stopped the war?" Luci frowned. She stared at Fahd as he shook his head, then waited quietly for him to reply. The wheels bumped and burred across patches of hard sand, shushing again in the softer, deeper parts, the tips of dune tongues licking at the tyres of the battered Toyota transporting an English rose and a Libyan panther across the desert wastes.

"I stopped Basma," Fahd said. He looked at Luci, adding, "I stopped my sister."

Fahd slowed for a steep decline, pointing to a crest of black rocks lit by the moon. He said nothing more until the Toyota was safely on firm ground at the bottom of a dune and in the mouth of a gully. The scent of something tart and wet drifted into the cab through the open windows, tickling Luci's nostrils with a brush of night wind. Fahd lit a cigarette, and Luci smiled at the thought of sharing a cigarette with Joci in the thunderbox, and how very far away and incredibly long ago it seemed, although it was little more than a week since she had said goodbye to her sister in Manchester Airport.

Fahd has a sister, Luci thought, wondering if they would ever meet. The look on Fahd's face suggested it was unlikely as he continued the story.

"She said she was fighting for our country and our freedom. I said she was self, *self…*" He shook his head as if searching for the word.

"Selfish?" Luci whispered, daring to put words in Fahd's mouth.

"Yes," he said, nodding his thanks. "She did not agree. We argued. I said she should think of our parents – too old to run if the militias came for them."

"The militias?"

"Does it matter?" Fahd shrugged. "There were many. Basma opposed them, the ones in support of the suppression of women. *That* I could understand, but family…" Fahd paused. "In war, family is all one has. I did not want to lose them. I did not want to lose her. We argued some more. She grabbed her gun. She walked out. I reached for her…" Fahd reached out to curl his hands gently around Luci's arm. She felt the emotion tremble through his fingers. Even though his touch was light, she saw the look in his eyes, knew then that he had been rough with his sister, that she had been rough with him. "I caught her," he said, letting go of Luci's arm. "She tried to pull free. She could not. I have always been stronger. We used to wrestle as kids. She never beat me unless I let her. She knew this. She pushed the gun towards me. Her finger was on the trigger. And when I slapped the barrel of the gun down, like this…" Fahd slapped the steering wheel and Luci jumped in her seat. "She pulled the trigger. She shot her foot."

"She shot *her* foot?"

Fahd nodded.

"I called for help. She didn't want it. I tried to stay. She told me to go. She never wanted to see me again." He shrugged again. "This was the price."

"The price of what?"

"For her to leave the war, to stop fighting. She lost three toes that day. She will always walk with a limp. But…" Fahd paused to finish his cigarette. "She is alive today. Our parents are alive. We are still family. Although…"

"You never see her," Luci said.

Fahd nodded. "The price," he said.

Luci slumped in the passenger seat, snatching glances at Fahd, smiling when he caught her, laughing when he smiled back, but saying nothing. She had nothing *to* say. English suburban life paled in comparison to the struggle for freedom and family in Libya.

"Ah," Fahd said as he slowed the HiLux to a stop. "We have arrived."

"This is it?" Luci peered into the night but saw little more than a ridge of black rocks brushed by sand like a tide lapping at the shore.

"It is a cave," Fahd said as he opened the driver's door. "I have flashlights. We will crawl inside tonight. You will want to see what is on the walls."

"The walls? Fahd?" Luci called out as Fahd

climbed out of the Toyota. He clambered up the ladder at the rear of the vehicle and tossed a small pack onto the sand. "Are we going to sleep in the cave?"

"It is comfortable," Fahd said. "We could sleep in there."

He grabbed a second pack and tossed it beside the first before jumping down. Luci watched as Fahd found two flashlights, checked they were working, and then pressed one of them into Luci's hand.

"Are you cold?" he asked when she shivered at his touch.

"Not cold," she said. Luci nodded at the rocks. "I'll follow you."

Fahd grinned and then flashed the beam over a small crack between two large boulders. "It's this way," he said.

Luci waited a second and then cast a look up at the stars, wondering not for the first time what Joci might say if she could see her now.

"More importantly," she whispered. "What would Joci do next?"

Big sisters, even those just a few minutes older, were supposed to lead the way, but it was not Joci but Fahd who Luci followed into the cave in the middle of the Libyan sands. She laughed at a second shiver of something that could have been *fear*, might have been *excitement*, but, in truth, was probably a shiver of *expectation*, although Luci was the first to admit she had no idea what to expect of Fahd, herself, or what lay waiting inside the cave.

"Just do it," she said, as she took a purposeful stride after Fahd and followed him inside the cave.

Fahd reached for Luci's pack as she pushed it in front of her. He took it from her, and then took her free hand, drawing her gently into the cave.

"Watch your head," he said. "The first part is low." Fahd's voice echoed inside the cave and Luci shivered again, this time from the cold air that hung heavily on the other side of the crack. Fahd tugged a thin duvet jacket out of Luci's pack and helped her put it on once she could stand. "There is a lot of room," he said as Luci slipped her sleeves inside the jacket. "You can stand now, and far into the cave."

"It's like a tunnel," she said as she clutched the flashlight under one arm to zip the jacket. She thought her breath was steaming in the light but realised it was dust motes floating in the air.

"This way," Fahd said, offering Luci his hand, and then, clasping it warmly, he led her deeper inside the cave.

Gone was the soft velvet desert night, but the walls of the cave were no less magical, and when the beam of Fahd's flashlight settled on the first drawing, Luci sensed the magic of the place – strong enough to take her breath away.

"But they're…"

Fahd grinned as he played the light over a series of crude drawings of figures carrying spears, chasing – or being chased by – large beasts with and without horns, some with four legs, others just two.

"These are…"

"People," Fahd said. He let go of Luci's hand and directed the beam of her flashlight to join his, pointing here, drifting there, bringing light to the scene of the hunt, following the flight of the humans, capturing the moment of the hunt when the beast was killed – thin, crooked spears protruding from its crudely daubed form.

"Cave paintings."

"Yes."

"But humans came later. They didn't hunt dinosaurs."

"You're sure?" Fahd played his flashlight over more scenes, more hunting.

"They could be stories."

"How would they know to tell such stories?"

"They wouldn't," Luci said. "Unless…"

She turned her attention to the floor of the cave, crouched beside the ridges of something that protruded unnaturally from the floor as if they had been exposed, scraped away by tools.

"Mazin was here," Fahd said. "This is his cave." He directed the beam of his flashlight to an alcove in the rock ahead of them. "Come."

Luci followed and then pressed her hand to her mouth.

"See?" Fahd said.

Luci nodded, eyes wide. She *saw*.

Just as Sugar had suggested, Lesothosaurus – fully formed, pressed into the rock like a painting, but with such exquisite detail it could only be bones, exposed when a slab of rock cracked and split from the face inside the cave.

"Here." Fahd turned his beam on another section. "Mazin removed some with a chisel. Others had fallen with time – many, *many* years ago. It's why he knew to look. It's why the people told their stories." Fahd shone the light back on the cave paintings. "Maybe they didn't hunt beasts in the desert. Only in here," he said, tapping the side of his head.

"Yes," Luci said. "I see."

She took a step closer to the Lesothosaurus preserved in the rock wall in front of her and then blinked in a sudden harsh light as Fahd turned on the lamps Mazin and his team had left in the cave.

"There is food and water," he said. "Even field cots. Mazin slept in here. He did not wish to be parted from his…"

"I can understand why," Luci said. She turned when she realised Fahd had not finished his sentence. "Fahd?"

"Shush," he said, pressing a finger to his lips. "Do you hear it?"

"The soldiers?" Luci shivered again and then gripped the flashlight. "Did they find the car?"

"Wait here," Fahd said. He walked along the cave towards the entrance.

"I'm coming with you," Luci said. She took Fahd's hand before he could argue that she should stay, and gripped it just as tightly as she held the flashlight, walking with Fahd all the way to the crack in the rock. She let go when he said he was going to look outside. "Okay," she whispered.

Fahd got no further than the crack. He stayed inside the cave mouth, shaking his head slightly, before looking up.

"Fahd?" Luci said. "What's that crackling sound?"

"I don't know," Fahd said as he squirmed back into the cave. "There is something in the sky. Sometimes, when it is very quiet, you can hear a shooting star, like a firework, crackling across the sky. I don't know. Maybe it is a star. Maybe that is just another story, but I think we should stay inside the cave tonight."

"But we could just..." Luci pointed at the Toyota.

"No," Fahd said. "Mazin has left us everything we need." He took another look at the opening and then pointed the beam of his flashlight back the way they had come. "We should go deeper into the cave. The rock is thick. It will protect us."

"Protect us?" Luci reached for Fahd as he stepped around her. "From what? What's out there, Fahd? And," she started, not really wanting to ask, "what are you afraid of?"

"I might be afraid," Fahd said. "Not often. And never in the desert. But tonight..."

"Fahd?"

"Come," he said, reaching for Luci's hand. "Come away from the entrance. We will rest. We will look outside in the morning. Not now. Not for a while."

Luci turned for another look at the cave entrance, resisting the tug of Fahd's fingers, until another shiver urged her to follow him deeper into the cave, out of the starlight.

15

Jazzman found Jay in the guard tower above the gate. He whistled before climbing the ladder mounted on the side of the Hesco wall and then started to climb when Jay waved him up. A soft, warm wind blew the dust off the top of the wall, curling in white waves as the moonlight caught it. Jazzman pointed at it and sat down next to Jay.

"Reminds me of a beach we once knew," he said as he dug a thermos flask and two enamel mugs out of the satchel he wore slung across his chest.

"That was a long time ago," Jay said. He nodded when his friend offered him coffee. They clinked their mugs together, then sat quietly through the first few sips. The camp buzzed below them, humming with the generators, the rustle of loose canvas, and Sparrow's excitable whoops and shouts, followed by Marion's repeated calls for him to *calm the fuck down*. Jazzman shook his head and laughed when he caught Jay's eye.

"This is some next level shit we've landed ourselves in this time, boss."

"It is," Jay said.

Jazzman paused, waiting for Jay to say more, and then pushed on regardless. "I noticed you walked out of the briefing."

"You noticed that, eh?"

"I did." Jazzman topped up his coffee. "I was wondering…"

"Why I walked out?" Jay snorted, then ran a hand around his beard, plucking at the sand as he talked. "Well, let's just say, even if I believed it…"

"Which you don't?"

"What I don't believe," Jay said, "is that that's what this is all about." He gestured at the desert inside the perimeter with a wave of his hand. "Is that really why we're here? Because some billionaire wants to create *Jurassic Sandbox*? I mean, really?"

"I don't know about that, boss. But Adler's not a billionaire."

"He's not?"

"Nope."

Jay turned to rest his back against the side of the guard tower. "Then what the hell is he?"

"Word is, he's with some kind of government think tank." Jazzman nodded when Jay shook his head. "It's true. The German lady said so, and she doesn't strike me as the type to lie."

"Ulli? What did she say?"

"Well, after you left, and the briefing was over, she told the rest of us about how she was contacted for a special job. It needed to be done fast. Apparently, when Adler told her what he needed, she refused. Said it couldn't be done. That Hesco was good, that it could take a pounding, but not a repeated pounding – which is what he said it might have to cope with. She said Adler told her it had to withstand a collision with a truck. She wanted to know if the truck was carrying a bomb. He said it wasn't. So…" Jazzman paused for a sip of coffee. "She says she could probably do it, seeing as the raw materials are here, but it would need a lot of Hesco, and supplies were limited. Adler assured he could get what she needed, provided she had the team to build it."

"She did." Jay gestured at the wall. "Obviously."

"Right, but when she pressed him about these hypothetical trucks slamming into the wall…"

"The dinosaurs?" Jay said with another shake of his head.

"Yep. Prehistoric beasts brought back from the dead. Although he didn't tell her that at the time. She had to sign a shit-tonne of NDAs before he would even tell her where it was to be built and how long she had to build it. Anyway…" Jazzman offered Jay more coffee, then stuck the thermos back in his satchel. "Adler said the wall just had to withstand a few knocks the first few days, after which it would be unlikely there would be any more activity."

"What? Are you saying these things are going to die? Or is it our job to put them down?"

"Hey, don't look at me, boss. I'm just telling you what she said. Besides, Marion sent me up here to tell you you've got a data packet waiting, and it's your eye only. Singular. As in…"

"Retinal scan." Jay scratched at another crust

of sand in his beard. He stood up and said, "I guess I'll go down and see what it's all about, eh?"

"Sure," Jazzman said. "You do that, and I'll keep an eye out for any funky shit going down in the desert."

"You're not worried about the radiation?"

"The guy, Adler, said they nuked Utah, right?"

"He did."

"Well, last I heard, Utah's doing fine." Jazzman shrugged. "I saw the map. Whatever they're gonna beam into the desert is happening way over there." He pointed. "And I ain't moving."

"Got it," Jay said.

"Of course, I did wonder about the comprehensive health package."

"Yeah…"

"And now our German engineer has me wondering that if whatever Adler is reviving… If it's just gonna keel over and die a couple of days after it's come back, then what the hell is the point?"

"I have no idea."

"And," Jazzman said, as Jay stepped onto the top rung of the ladder. "How does it work, anyway? These ceti particles, man… Are they really gonna bring back the dead? What kind of science is that? It sounds all kinds of extra-terrestrial to me. Like some funky outer space shit."

"Don't overthink it," Jay said with a nod to

Jazzman. "You'll go mad, you know?"

He slid down the ladder before Jazzman could respond and then headed for the team room. Marion pointed at a ruggedized laptop on the table when he stepped inside.

"Is Ulli still here?" Jay asked.

"The engineer?" Marion shook her head. "She and her buddy took off to plug the gap in the wall. Adler said she had until midnight."

"Right."

Marion took a step closer and lowered her voice. "Sparrow's more hyper than usual. I can't figure out if he's genuinely excited, or a little freaked out."

"You mean, scared?" Jay frowned. "That doesn't sound like Sparrow."

"No, but..." Marion licked her lip as if considering her next words carefully. "But after what that guy just told us. This is some..."

"Next level shit?" Jay smiled. "Jazzman just told me."

"And you walked out on us..."

"No, I walked out on *him*," Jay said, pointing at the sender's name on the encrypted email. He took a breath and then checked his watch. "Listen. It's still early. Why don't you take Sparrow down to the southeast corner, check on the engineers, and then come back here by twenty-three-hundred hours? We can chill in the team room while Adler beams whatever the hell he's going to beam down into the desert. It'll all make a lot more sense in the morning."

"Sure, but, boss..."

"Yeah?"

"Is this some Christmas Island, shit? Are we guinea pigs, or something? Is that why the health comp was so good? Or do they think we're going to get torn up by some prehistoric monster with a million year old hangover?"

Jay nodded and said, "Something like that, I guess." He pointed at the door. "Get Sparrow. Take Scruffette with you. She likes the night, right?"

Marion nodded.

"See you in a couple hours," Jay said. He waited until she was gone and then fished a set of wireless earbuds out of his vest pocket. He stuffed them in his ears and then pressed his eye close to the camera for the required scan to unlock the file. He checked he was alone and then opened it. Adler's face filled the screen as if he was fiddling with the camera, and then retreated as the older man – *not* a billionaire – took a step back.

"Mr Styles," Adler said. "*Warbird*, if I may?"

"You may," Jay whispered to himself.

"You and your team come highly recommended. And, given your previous experience, it is our opinion – mine, and my colleagues – that you have the necessary skills to carry out this mission."

Adler paused, and Jay wondered if he was going to say *if you choose to accept it*. But Adler clicked an image of what looked like a DNA helix into the video and Jay reached for a chair and sat down.

"As you know, *Reviver* is a very special,

astronomically expensive, and rather radical experiment. Nothing quite like it has ever been tried or even conceptualised before. It came about as a result of a very broad brief, for a group to consider the future of warfare and the demands that will place on a society such as ours, which simply has no stomach for war. I am part of a small group charged with exploring that brief and providing solutions at any cost. And, in the case of *Reviver*, that cost is massive." Adler paused to slide another image onto the screen next to the first one.

"You have got to be kidding me." Jay reached for a non-existent stiff drink and then settled for a sip of water from the bottle in his vest.

"These specimens are the real prize of *Reviver*," Adler said as he continued. "They are Phase Two. Phase One is the operational delivery of the ceti particles. Phase Two is containment and capture. These specimens are your number one priority, Mr Styles. There is no secondary mission. Once the package has been delivered, you and your team will track DNA flares identified by the same satellite delivery system and beamed to your location. It is very important that the specimens are secured and retrieved as quickly as possible. Once you have the specimens – at least one of each sex – your task will be to deliver them to an agreed extraction point. Once Phase Two is complete, Phase Three will be initiated."

"Phase Three?" Jay whispered. "There's

another fucking phase?"

"You're wondering what Phase Three is, aren't you, Mr Styles?" Adler's face reappeared on the screen as the images of the specimens disappeared. He took a breath and then looked directly at the camera. "Ceti particles bring life to the dead, Mr Styles. But the gamma radiation they are delivered upon is lethal. While we can treat the specimens if you get them to us in time – hence the critical nature of finding and securing them within a window of forty-eight hours or less – it is anticipated that any other life forms revived by the ceti particles, will degrade and ultimately die before they pose too great a problem. Phase Three is the mopping up operation, in which you and your team will destroy all remaining life forms, including any of the specimens identified in Phase Two." Adler paused and then said, "Everything dies, Mr Styles. Everything."

"Jesus…"

Jay listened with just one ear, catching words such as *helicopter gunships available* and *high explosive ordnance*, while another part of his brain considered the implications of finding Adler's specimens, and further thoughts about what he might do with them, and, not least, how they might fit into Adler's thoughts about the future of warfare.

"… of course, you have a pilot on your team," Adler said as Jay tuned back into the briefing. "But we don't want to panic the specimens more than absolutely necessary. If you have to get them out on foot, that's what you do."

On foot?

Adler's briefing ended abruptly, and Jay leaned back in his chair. He took a breath as he tried to process the ins and outs of the mission he had just been tasked with until a new email popped into his inbox. Jay frowned as the sender's name was withheld and the subject was California. Jay clicked on the mail, wondering if it was from Malcolm, and if he had found a suitable care home for Jay's mother.

But the content of the mail was nothing more than a link to a message service, a one-time password, and a short note that read: WE NEED TO TALK.

"Okay," Jay said. "As if my day couldn't get any weirder."

Jay clicked the link, entered the password, and then peered at the screen as a vaguely familiar face flickered into focus.

"Warbird?"

"Beane?" Jay said. "What the hell?"

"Are you secure?"

"Sure."

"Are you alone?"

Jay nodded and then looked up. "It's just me."

"Where are you, Jay?"

"I'm in the fucking desert, man," Jay said.

Beane looked away and swore. When he looked back, he was all business. "Okay, Jay," he said. "This is what you need to know."

PART
III

16

Haines tossed in her sleep with every step she took towards the Utahraptor. It was green and black until she remembered the night vision goggles. Haines bumped her husband with her elbow as she mimed the action of removing the goggles in her dreams, oblivious to his shout, the moving of the bed as he rubbed his eye, and then Bill's hand as he tried to shake her awake.

"Warren."

She pushed them away – whoever they were. Haines thought they must be some of Beane's men, cautioning her, telling her to be wary of the beast, that it wasn't quite dead, and that *not-quite-dead* was far more deadly, one hundred percent lethal, in fact, than a live animal in the best of health.

"It's not an animal," Haines said, clear now, nodding in her sleep, still trying to push Beane's man away. "It's a raptor. A dinosaur – back from the dead."

"That's it."

Bill Haines threw the covers back and rolled out of bed. He fumbled for the light switch – caught it, flicked it on – and bathed the room in light.

"Hey…" Haines raised her hand, suddenly

awake as the light burned through her eyelids and the Utahraptor retreated deeper behind the rocks in the desert gully outside Vernon. "What are you doing, Bill?"

"What am *I* doing?"

"What time is it?"

Bill rubbed his eyes and looked at the clock. "A little after three."

"In the morning?"

"Yes, Warren, it's morning. Really early in the morning. And for the sixth night in a row, you've woken me up with an elbow in the eye."

"God. Bill," Haines said, reaching for her husband. "I did that?"

"Yeah," he said. Bill sat down on the side of the bed. He straightened his boxer shorts, smiled sleepily when Haines ran her hand over his generous belly. "It's been rough these past few nights. Feels like I've been fighting with one of those dinosaurs you keep dreaming about."

"Dinosaurs?"

"Yeah, I don't know, babe. Some kind of raptor. I thought you were losing it a little, and then there was that guy on TV."

"What guy?" Haines said, suddenly awake. She sat up and reached for Bill's hand. "Tell me."

"What? About the guy who thinks he saw a dinosaur in the desert?" Bill laughed. "You haven't seen it?"

"No."

"It's on all the channels. Maybe less so now, but a week ago it was the only thing they talked about on local news. Apparently, a couple of dogs and some chickens went missing. Then some kid got out his big book of dinosaurs and identified the damn thing. That got the attention of the usual crowd, and one palaeontologist who took him seriously and drove all the way out from California to interview the kid." Bill shook his head. "You haven't seen this?"

"If it's not on CNN or Fox, or…"

"Right," Bill said. "You know, there's a world outside of D.C., babe. You know that?"

"I know."

Haines slipped out of bed, tugged her pyjama top over her waist and headed for the door.

"You're getting up?"

"I'm awake," Haines said. "I'll make coffee." She stopped, one hand on the door, and said, "This is one of those few weekends free. You know it gets crazy in the fall. If we have an early start, we can get more out of the weekend."

"Yeah, I guess," Bill said. "Just don't wake Tessa," he said, as he flopped back on the bed.

Haines promised she wouldn't, and then snuck out of the bedroom, biting her lip to stop her swearing as she stubbed her toe on the leg of the dresser in the hall. Bill was supposed to move it into the spare room a month earlier, but then decided he liked it where it was.

"And you're not home enough to argue," he had said when Haines complained about it.

Stalemate.

And Haines didn't even play chess.

She limped to the bathroom, peed, and then pulled on a housecoat before climbing down the creaky stairs to the kitchen. Haines smiled as she spooned a generous portion of Colombian coffee granules into the coffee machine and then grabbed her smartphone.

"Beane?" she said when he answered. "So, I know it's early. And I'm okay. But…"

"What's going on, ma'am?" Beane grunted, still not awake.

"Bill knows about the raptor. It was in the paper and all over the news, apparently."

"Yeah, I know."

"And you didn't tell me?" Haines walked from the kitchen to the living room as Beane grunted something about it being *nothing to worry about*. She stopped at the window, spreading her fingers to open a slat in the blind. "Well, if you say so."

"Listen," Beane said. He cleared his throat, and his voice came back stronger. "We've got other things to worry about."

"Is that why Claud's parked out front?"

"What's that?"

"Claud," Haines said. "Blonde hair. Blue eyes. Claud. She's parked in an SUV right outside my house."

"Right now?"

"Yes, Beane. Right this minute. I'm looking at her now." Haines took a breath and then remembered it was still early in the morning. "I'm sorry," she said. "I should let you sleep. Goodbye, Beane…"

"No, wait!"

Haines stopped with her thumb above the

screen and then pressed the phone to her ear. "What's that?"

"Don't hang up," Beane said.

Haines frowned at the sound of a thump, followed by a string of curses.

"Are you okay?"

"Dressing," Beane said. "Not very well."

"Okay…"

"I'm coming over."

"Now? Why?"

"Listen carefully, Warren."

Haines pinched her housecoat as the urgency in Beane's voice, and his use of her first name sent an unexpected shiver through her body. She stepped away from the window.

"Beane?"

"Claud's supposed to be on a job in Mexico," he said. "I took her off your protection team and gave her the assignment south of the border."

"Why?"

"Because she's getting too chummy with Adler."

"I don't understand," Haines said. "What has that got to do with…" Haines swallowed. "Oh…"

"Right," Beane said. "Loose ends. Adler can't have any." Beane paused as if he was wondering how much to say, and then came back on the line more urgent than ever. "This isn't a secure line, but fuck it, we're way past secure now, Senator."

"And now you're scaring me, Beane."

"Who's in the house?"

"Bill… Tessa," Haines said.

"Get them into the bathroom. Lock the door. Barricade it if you can…"

"Beane?"

"And get in the tub – all three of you."

"Beane for God's sake. It's *Claud*. You know? Your friend. The one who lends me her shoes all the time."

"Get in the tub, Warren. I'll be right over. Ten minutes. Max."

"Beane…"

The line went dead and Haines clutched the phone to her chest. The Haines' household was in a quiet neighbourhood, with no early risers that Haines knew of, and few commuters up before five or six in the morning. A hush fell over the house, with the percolating coffee the only sound.

"Warren?"

Haines jumped at the sound of her name and looked up just as Bill trudged down the stairs in his boxer shorts and his favourite t-shirt with a large, faded *Route 66* stencilled on the front.

"Who were you talking to?"

"Beane," Haines said. "My protection."

"Yes?"

She took a breath, nodded a few times and then said, "He wants us to wake Tessa and lock ourselves in the bathroom."

"What?"

"Yes," Haines said. "And we should get in the bathtub. All three of us. Together."

"He wants us to do what?" Bill shook his head. "Is this for real?"

"Yes." Haines nodded. "We should wake

Tessa."

"I'll wake Tessa. If we're in danger, you should get your…" Bill stopped talking as someone turned a key in the lock of the front door. "Warren?"

"Go get Tessa," she shouted. Haines stuffed her phone into the pocket of her housecoat and then ran for the door. She thrust her weight against it and slid the safety chain across it, amazed that a part of her brain actually chided her for not putting Bill on the door. He was heavier, stronger, and might even buy a few more minutes.

"Senator?"

Haines froze as she recognised Claud's voice on the other side.

"Yes?"

"Are you holding the door?"

"Yes," Haines said. "Why?"

"I heard something," Claud said. "I was parked outside. I was on my way in to check if everything was all right."

"Everything's fine," Haines said. "I had a nightmare. I got up. I made coffee."

"Okay." Claud tried the handle again. "I should come in and check," she said.

Haines stopped herself from saying *no, you should be in Mexico*. And then Bill was behind her on the stairs, hissing her name until she turned her head.

"Tessa's in the bathroom," he said. "Scared out of her mind."

"Yes."

"Is that Bill you're talking to, Senator?"

"Yeah, Bill's here," Haines said. And then, before she thought better of it, she said, "And Beane's on his way."

"Beane?"

Haines swallowed as Claud paused.

The coffee machine beeped.

And then Haines turned her head sharply at the sound of Claud unsnapping a Velcro tab she guessed secured the pistol in her holster.

"You called him? Senator?"

"Yes," Haines breathed.

"I wish you hadn't done that," Claud said. "There was no reason to do that."

Haines wondered how long it had been since Beane hung up. Was it ten minutes? Was it five? Was it only three?

"Senator?"

"Yes?"

"You should probably step away from the door now."

"Why would I do that?"

"Because I'm coming in."

The front door of the Haines house was, as Beane described it, too thin to be a real deterrent, but nothing to worry about as he would have a team on the street whenever Haines was home. Beane even encouraged Haines to give him an extra set of keys for the teams in the event of a home invasion.

Claud had a key, but she didn't use it.

The Rhodium Security operative's first kick sent a tremor through the door that caught Haines by surprise. She fell backwards and then reached for the door again until Bill shouted that she should leave it.

"It was a warning," he said, pulling Haines to her feet and dragging her upstairs. "She's going to blow the lock off."

"She wouldn't…"

She did.

Claud fired three suppressed shots at the lock and then kicked it a second time, snapping the chain as the door swung open. She lifted the pistol, fired up the stairs and shot Bill in the thigh as he pushed Haines in front of him. Bill screamed and tumbled down the stairs. Claud waited for him to roll into the hall and stepped over him with a long, almost mechanical stride. She looked around the corner and fired again, putting a hole in the wall above Haines' head with a *phut* as the bullet passed through the suppressor.

"I'm not going to hurt your family, Senator," Claud said as she climbed the stairs. She paused and glanced at Bill writhing on the floor. "Well, I'm not going to hurt them unnecessarily. But, you see, you made it necessary when you had second thoughts. Mr Adler needs your support, Senator. Now, you could have walked away," Claud said as she climbed another step. "You could have backed out without a bad word and no hard feelings. But it seemed you and Beane developed some kind of goddamned ethical code all of a sudden. And Mr Adler can't have that. He can't have that at all."

Claud climbed the last stairs onto the landing and reached for the bathroom door.

Locked.

Claud sighed and then leaned against the wall as she changed magazines.

"Of course," she said, raising her voice above the whimper of a teenager inside the bathroom. "Calling Beane wasn't smart, but it could be convenient." She nodded as she thought about it. "If he comes here, I don't have to go looking for him. Which makes everything a lot easier," she said, turning her head at the sound of tyres squealing in the street outside the house. "And," she added, "a whole lot more fun."

Claud checked the bathroom door was still locked and then took a cautious step towards the top of the staircase.

17

Luci was the first to wake. She swung her legs over the side of the cot, checked her boots for scorpions, and then pulled them on, casting glances at Fahd as he slept on the cot on the other side of the cave. For all the glances and smiles they had swapped, all the magnetism, there was something unspoken between them, an understanding that whatever happened would happen when it happened and not before. Luci felt like a teenager again and smiled as she realised she liked it. She pulled on the duvet jacket and padded past the Lesothosaurus on the cave wall and made her way to the exit.

Whatever it was that had spooked Fahd in the night, encouraging him to make them stay inside the cave, seemed to have passed. Luci sensed nothing untoward in the air, tasted nothing strange on her tongue when she took her first breath outside the cave, and saw nothing immediately strange about the Toyota.

Although the sand looks a little lighter.

Luci tilted her head to one side as she caught sight of something green poking up through the sand. New growth, but rapid, as if there had been a trigger of some sort. She remembered the tart, damp taste of something in the night on the drive to the cave but had guessed it was a night flower or something similar, opening its fronds or petals to attract moisture or a meal depending upon its preferred choice of sustenance. But the green growth by the wheel looked like a fern, and on closer inspection Luci thought it looked like a very old kind of fern, the kind she had seen fossils of during the geology field trips she took when she was studying for her degree in East Anglia.

She crouched for a closer look, but as she bent down, she saw more shoots, some further on than others, and the unmistakable balls of leafy fronds uncurling.

She lifted her head and finally saw the metaphorical wood, not just the trees, as the fronds were everywhere. Some wilted in the early morning heat, while others, in the shade cast by the car and the rocks, reached for the sun.

There was more.

Tracks around the vehicle revealed activity that was either from a whole colony of desert mice or rats, perhaps joined by lizards, or something bigger and undecided, scampering back and forth with unsteady strides, leaving strange impressions in the sand.

"Not strange," Luci whispered as she crouched once more for a closer look. "I know these tracks." A lick of desert wind teased at her hair, and she brushed it to one side. Then, as she knelt on the sand, hands on either side of the tracks to really get a good look, Luci caught a flicker of movement and lifted her head to find it.

"Don't move," Fahd said as he padded across

the sand, panther-like, to stand behind her.

"What is it?" Luci whispered. She lifted her head another inch.

"Don't…"

Out of the corner of her eye, Luci saw what could have been a very large, leathery turkey, or a fat ostrich, even, because there was no way, no *possible* way, she could be looking at a Lesothosaurus.

And yet, as she lifted her head another inch, there was little doubt in her mind that she was, indeed, looking at the very dinosaur Sugar had sent her to the cave to find, although Luci was pretty sure Sugar had been talking about evidence, fossils, perhaps even bones and not a real, live Lesothosaurus.

"There's three," Fahd whispered. "One on your left. Two in front. Moving behind the car now."

"I see them," Luci said. "I'm going to stand up," she said.

"I don't know…"

"I do." Luci caught one of those embarrassed laughs in her throat, and gave Fahd a bewildered smile instead, before adding, "If you run, I want to run with you."

"You think we should run?"

Luci took a breath. The sun beat down on the dirty glass of the Toyota, and she blinked in the glare, turning her head again as she stood up, keeping her eye on the Lesothosauri.

"Plural," she said.

"What will they do?"

"How should I know?"

"You studied them."

"I studied the *evidence* of them." Luci turned her head slowly to look at Fahd. "It's conjecture, based on evidence combined with theory. We think the Lesothosaurus might have lived in packs, in burrows."

"They weren't in the cave," Fahd said. He looked at the entrance. "Maybe they want to go inside the cave? Maybe we should let them?"

"We could do that." Luci reached for Fahd's hand. It was silly, perhaps, but she needed to touch someone, something real. Luci's world had twisted in the night, and she needed to be grounded. She looked at the entrance to the cave as they stepped away from it, wondering if the cave was a magic cave.

The thought made her laugh."

"Luci," Fahd hissed.

"What?" She laughed again, and then let go of Fahd's hand to press one hand to her mouth, curling the other around her hip. She laughed for a third time. The laugh became a giggle, and suddenly, there, outside the cave, just a few feet away from a small herd, or a flock – they were ornithischians, after all – Fahd got it. He understood, and he smiled.

"They should be dead," he said.

"Yes."

"Perhaps we are dead. *Ow!*" he said, as Luci grabbed his hand and pinched him.

"Not dead," she said, taking his hand, pulling him gently and slowly away from the cave entrance. "Just really, *really* confused."

"Yes," he said, as the smallest Lesothosaurus dipped its long neck, turning its head and narrow beak just like a curious ostrich, studying them, before approaching the cave. Fahd and Luci stared at its leathery skin, whispered comments about how pale it was, how patchy, until the dinosaur was gone. It slipped inside the cave and the two larger beasts followed it just as quickly.

Fahd relaxed and then reached inside his trouser pockets for a crumpled packet of cigarettes. His fingers trembled as he lit one. He relaxed a little more as he took his first drag.

"How?" he said.

"I have no idea." Luci pointed at the vegetation around the vehicle and in the shadow and shade cast by the rocks. "I can't explain any of this. I mean, if there was a flash flood…"

"We would be dead," Fahd said. "There was no flood. The ground is bone dry." He sniffed the air and wrinkled his nose. "Is that smell… Is that them?"

Luci took a deep breath. Her nose twitched with the scent of something with a reptilian taint of dry skin, mixed with old musty feathers, slightly damp, and something darker that reminded her of death.

"Maybe," she said. "This is new. They are new." Luci said, pointing at the cave. "Meaning, they weren't here last night."

"They were not."

"And…" Luci stopped talking as the ground shook beneath their feet. She stepped to one side, and then, when Fahd flicked his cigarette on the ground and pointed to the rocks above the cave, she followed, running behind him until they reached the rocks and climbed to safety. "Quicksand?" she asked once she had recovered her breath.

"No," Fahd said. "There is no quicksand here. To the west, there is a patch I know, nearby, but this…" Fahd stopped talking as the ground crumbled, and slabs of packed sand splintered into dust. Rocks spilled out of the sand and onto the surface. The pebbles scattered furthest, striking the side of the car with dulls thuds and the occasional *pling* as the ground continued to crumble and heave, and from within, rising out of the ground was a head roughly half the size of Fahd. He gasped as the head continued its upward journey upon a long, thick neck. Fahd scrabbled backwards, reaching for Luci, pulling her with him as she grasped his hand.

"I don't know," Luci said. "Don't ask me. Because I don't know."

"But if you did? If you knew. If it was possible… Luci," Fahd said. "What it is?"

Luci knew what it *couldn't* be.

"It can't be…" she said.

"Can't be what?"

"It can't be a Rebbachisaurus," Luci said.

"And why *can't* it be?" Fahd shook his head as the dinosaur stumbled up and out of the ground with legs like palm trunks. It had a spiny sail on its back that moved as the dinosaur thumped forward, moving up, lifting its head, to rise and to *tower* above them. "Why can't it be what you said?"

"Because," Luci said as she scrabbled up the rocks, glancing over her shoulder at the dinosaur, stopping in the shelter of a depression in the sand, protected by a ring of black rocks, when Fahd pulled her into it. "Because it lived around 100 million years ago."

"Where?"

"Morocco," Luci said. "It was discovered in Morocco."

"To the west," Fahd said, nodding as if it suddenly made sense.

"The car," Luci said, pointing as the dinosaur found its feet – all four of them – and settled on the packed earth outside the cave. It lurched to one side, recovered with a swish of its tail, and then lurched back again. A second swing of the tail connected with the Toyota, batting it to one side, but without knocking it over.

"It's a HiLux," Fahd said with a grin. "It can survive anything."

"Look." Luci pointed as the Rebbachisaurus, similar in shape to the more familiar Diplodocus, extended its sail. "For balance?" Luci whispered. "Or…"

Luci turned her head to look across the desert behind them. From their vantage point on top of the rocks above the cave, the height afforded them a greater view, but even without the growing heat of the desert sun to distract and confuse them, there were simply too many *things* in the desert to be mirages.

"Luci…"

"Maybe it's for balance," Luci said, still thinking about the sail on the back of the Rebbachisaurus, all sixty-five of it. "Or maybe, like the books say…"

"What do the books say?" Fahd asked when Luci fell silent. "What do they say?"

Luci exhaled her breath in ragged steps as she pointed at a two-legged beast turning towards them. "They say it has a sail to intimidate predators."

"It's not a predator?"

"It's a herbivore," Luci said with a glance at the Rebbachisaurus as it plodded past them. "But that," she said, pointing at the dinosaur stumbling on two legs, as if, like everything thing else they had just witnessed, it was still finding its feet. "That's a predator," she said.

"And you know what that *can't* be, too?"

"Yes," Luci said as she stood up. "And I'll tell you what it isn't as soon as we are in the car."

"Good idea," Fahd said.

"Yes."

"Shall we run?"

"Definitely," Luci said. "We should definitely run."

Fahd led the way, picking a path down the rocks, pausing to check Luci was following, only to catch a frustrated look as she urged him on, pushing his shoulder when she caught up, pointing at the car as if it was the only thing that could save them.

"What about the cave? It can't fit in there."

"It's full of Lesothosaurus," Luci said.

"Herbivores," Fahd said.

"Frightened herbivores with teeth." Luci jumped the last few feet onto the sand and grabbed Fahd's arm. "You drive. I'll spot."

"Spot?"

"I'll look tell you what we shouldn't be seeing." She reached the Toyota, gripped the handle and yanked at the passenger door, until Fahd pointed out that it was buckled, but the windows were down.

"Crawl inside," he said as the ground trembled around them. "Hurry!"

Luci reached for the roof rack, grabbed it and clambered up the side of the car as Fahd ran around to the driver's side. Luci slid in through the passenger window. Fahd climbed behind the wheel. The Tyrannosaurus Rex – the dinosaur Luci simply knew it couldn't be – rounded the corner of the gully as Fahd turned the key in the ignition.

"Fahd."

"Yes."

"Fahd, it's close."

"I know."

"You have to hurry."

Luci pressed herself into the seat, bracing one hand on the door, and the other against Fahd's seat. She screamed. Fahd screamed with her, and the T-Rex roared – short, sharp, but loud enough to mask the sound of the HiLux' engine as it finally, *miraculously*, caught, and Fahd crunched into first gear, spinning the vehicle away from the cave and charging up the incline they had descended the previous night.

One night.

One hundred, maybe two hundred million years into the future.

"Fahd!"

"Yes," he said, wrestling the Toyota up the sandy hill.

"It's coming."

18

The first Rhodium patrol pulled out of camp in the midday heat. Jay drove the Humvee with Jazzman on the 50. calibre machine gun in the roof, Marion nursing Scruffette with battery-powered fans in the back, and Sparrow fiddling with one of the new Gruber 50. calibre pistols in the passenger seat. Jay told him to put it away.

"Before you go blind," he said.

"Sure, boss." Sparrow holstered the Gruber and then tugged his smartphone out of his vest pocket. "How about some tunes for our jolly in the sand?"

"Go ahead," Jay said. He looked to both sides, checking the two dodgems with the side-mounted rocket launchers were on each flank, and then nodded as Sparrow's *tunes* blasted through the speaker.

"Led Zeppelin?" Marion shouted from the back. "Really?"

"*Immigrant Song*, man," Sparrow said. "Totally appropriate."

Jay increased speed, forging a path across the hard-packed sand. The two dodgems fell in behind. Jazzman ducked into the cab for a bottle of water, flashing the thumbs up at Sparrow for his choice of music.

"I knew you'd like it, old man," Sparrow shouted back. "It's your era!"

"Not quite, you little punk." Jazzman shook his head and then took his position behind the .50.

Jay pushed the Humvee a little harder, clicking his fingers for Sparrow to concentrate on the screen. "The second you get a hit," he said, raising his voice above the music. "You vector us in."

"Got it."

"And what about us?" Marion said, leaning forward. "Rhodium told me we might need a cadaver dog in the desert, but I have no idea why."

"We might," Jay said, guessing that the specimens he was tasked to find might smell like death. *Or death warmed up,* he thought. He turned to Marion and said, "Makes sense, actually. Keep her cool."

"Working on it."Marion sank back into her seat and stroked Scruffette's ears.

They continued for another four miles, bumping over uneven patches of old roads, slowing as they crossed the softer stretches, and then cursing their way through deeper drifts and the tongues of long dunes. Sparrow shifted his gaze between the screen on the dash and the playlist on his smartphone. Jay waved one of the dodgems on ahead and then slammed on the brakes when the dodgem skidded to a sudden halt and Jazzman thumped on the roof.

"Contact right," Jazzman said, his voice cutting through the music a second before

Sparrow paused the playlist.

"Say again," Jay said. "I see nothing."

"You'll see it." Jazzman swore. "I mean, you can't miss it."

"Miss what?" Sparrow opened the passenger door and stepped out. "I don't see…"

"You see it now?" Jazzman said.

"Yeah," Sparrow said. "I see it." He turned back to Jay and laughed. "Do you know what that is?" Sparrow grinned. "It's a freaking *Spinosaurus*. I mean, I *know* what that is."

"And how the hell do you know that?" Jazzman said as the sixty-foot-long dinosaur – head to tail – strode on two legs less than one hundred feet to the team's right. He swore as the dinosaur turned its head towards them.

"Were you ever a kid?" Sparrow asked the older man. "You never went through the whole dinosaur phase?" Sparrow pointed at the dinosaur. "See the sail on its back?"

"We see it," Jay said. "Struggling to believe it."

"Well…" Sparrow shrugged and turned back to the team. "Yeah, I don't remember what it's for, or anything else, except it's a carnivore."

"Really?" Jay pointed at the Spinosaurus. "You're saying that ugly beast, the one looking at us right now, is a meat eater?"

"Yeah," Sparrow said with a nod. "That's exactly what I'm saying."

"Sparrow," Jazzman said as he primed the machine gun. "Get back in the Humvee."

"What?"

"Get in the fucking vehicle," Jay shouted. "Now!"

Sparrow turned as the Spinosaurus started to run. He swore, scrambled into the cab, and bumped the resume icon on the playlist as he tossed his phone onto the dashboard. More heavy metal tunes thrashed out of the Humvee's speakers as Jazzman shouted for instructions. Jay stuffed the Humvee into gear and accelerated, churning a plume of sand from the rear of the vehicle as he headed for the Rhodium dodgem in front of them.

"Still coming, boss," Jazzman shouted. "Orders?"

"Light him up," Jay shouted.

"Got it!"

Jazzman opened up with the .50 calibre machine gun. Tracer fire arced across the sand as small pyrotechnic charges ignited every three rounds, giving Jazzman a visual aid to zero in on the dinosaur. The first rounds slammed into the side of the Spinosaurus, giving it pause for a second or two as it stumbled to the left.

"You got it," Sparrow said from the passenger seat. "Hit it again."

Jazzman responded with another sustained burst and the cab echoed with the *thud thud thud* of the heavy machine gun.

"He's not stopping," Jazzman said. "This isn't going to stop him."

"Knock that music off," Jay said, as he accelerated. "Sparrow!"

"Yeah, I got it."

Sparrow killed the music at the same time as Jazzman stopped firing. Jay grabbed the radio and called up the dodgems.

"What are you carrying on the sides of your vehicles?"

A burst of static filled the cab, followed by the driver's response from the lead dodgem. "Hellfire missiles, sir."

"Hit it," Jay said. "Hit it hard."

Jay drove around the dodgem as the driver positioned the vehicle for a better shot.

"This'll be fun," Sparrow said. "Those missiles have been tweaked so any idiot can use them. If they miss…"

The first two missiles burst out of the side-mounted launchers. The exhaust mixed with the sand, enveloped the tiny bubble-canopied vehicle for a second, until the exhaust from two more rockets made it disappear completely.

"Holy shit!" Sparrow thumped the side of the Humvee as three of the rockets slammed into the side of the Spinosaurus, exploding in a geyser of prehistoric skin, blood, and bone, while the fourth sailed over the dinosaur's head to explode on a dune behind it.

"I guess Rhodium has employed idiots," Jay said once the dust had settled. "The rockets worked."

"Yeah," Sparrow said, his voice tailing off. "I guess they did."

Jazzman ducked into the cab, nodded at Jay, and then reached for Sparrow's shoulder. "You about done grieving?"

"What?"

Jazzman pointed out of the driver's window. "Multiple contacts. More childhood monsters come to fuck with you." He slapped Jay on the shoulder and said, "I'll be on the .50."

"Go," Jay said. He reached for the radio and declared *weapons free* before stuffing the Humvee into first and feathering the gas pedal. "Ready?"

"Wait," Sparrow said. He fiddled with the screen on the dash. "We're getting a signal."

"Where?"

"North," Sparrow said. "Northeast. Two klicks." He looked at Jay and said, "A little over a mile."

Jay nodded, reached for the radio again and gave the order for the dodgems to return to base.

"We might need them, boss," Marion said from the back seat.

"Understood, but we can't have them." Jay waited for the dodgems to retreat and then accelerated, veering north and then northeast whenever the terrain allowed. He thumped the roof, giving Jazzman the signal to drop down into the cab. "We are officially in Phase Two of the mission." He waited until he was sure he had their attention, encouraging them to ignore the multiple contacts visible to all sides, however difficult that might be. "Listen up," he said. "That blip on the screen is a DNA flare. It's our target."

"What kind of DNA, boss?" Marion asked.

"Human." Jay turned his head to look at each of them for a second. "Old human. You could say the first humans. At least, that's what that guy Adler is hoping for."

"Humans brought back from the dead?"

"Yeah…"

"Shit," Jazzman said. "And what's to say they're not…" He paused to consider his words. "What if they're more recent?"

"Adler only wants the old ones."

"And how are we going to know?"

"He assured me we'll know. And," Jay said, pointing at the screen, "he said the satellite can identify the humans we need, sorting their DNA from the ones we don't."

"It can read DNA from space?"

Jay gave Sparrow a hard stare and said, "What am I? A scientist?"

"No, boss."

"That's right," Jay said. "I'm just a grunt following orders. They've given us a signal, we drive to it, load the cargo and hightail it to the extraction point."

"Humans?"

"Yes, Maid. *Humans*."

"Then the dinosaurs?"

"I have no idea," Jay said. "And even if I did, we can never talk about it. So it stays here. In the desert. You want to talk about it? Talk to me. No one else."

"Boss…" Jazzman said.

Jay ignored him, raising his finger as he continued. "We knew what we were getting into. Rhodium never pays this kind of money for a gig, and they certainly wouldn't pay me a dime more than they could get away with, but…"

"Boss!"

"What?"

"Contact."

Jazzman thrust his arm between the seats and pointed at two naked humans covered in dust and blood. Jay slammed on the brakes and the Humvee slewed to a stop.

"How…?"

"I don't know." Jay took a breath. "Adler said something about the ceti particles in the data packet. Something about the *little bang*, like the *big bang theory*, only…" He licked at the dust on his lips and said, "Smaller."

"These cells," Marion said, shushing Scruffette as she whined. "They *revive* dead cells. That's what he said. So I'm guessing the life is germinated by a little bang, and then accelerated somehow." She cursed as the mental effort painted a frown across her brow. "I mean, it's one thing to think about dinosaurs, but…"

"This is different," Sparrow said. "I know…"

"No, you don't," Jay said, after a moment's pause. "You know nothing. This is *not* different. This is our target. This is why we're here."

"Boss?"

"No more questions or theories, Maid," Jay said, turning in his seat. "I want you and Sparrow to get out there, restrain them, and bring them back to the Humvee. Put them in the rear."

"Boss, don't…"

"Marion!" Jay reached for the front of her tactical vest and jerked her forward. "This is the mission. We get it done, we go home. These are humans. How old they are, and how they got here, doesn't matter. You get out there. Secure them. Bring them back." He let go of her vest and jabbed his finger at the dusty humans staggering towards them. "It looks like they're blinded. Get them before they open their eyes. Okay? Sparrow?"

"We're on it," Sparrow said. He turned to nod at Marion and then opened the door. The humans flinched at the sound. Marion cursed and then opened her door to follow Sparrow. Scruffette cowered on the back seat.

"And what about them?" Jazzman asked as he pointed at two more humans wandering towards them. He peered at them. "It looks like they're wearing clothes, Jay."

"Yeah, I see that."

"Tattered, but modern clothes, I guess."

"Shit." Jay opened the driver's door and stepped out. He ducked back inside to look at Jazzman. "Are you coming?"

"What are you going to do?"

"Adler said nothing else gets out. These guys have been dead once. They can't live again. Plus, they won't live that long – too much radiation."

"But we could save them?"

Jay shook his head. He pointed at the naked humans in front of Sparrow and Marion. "We save *them*. They're the mission."

"But, boss…"

"Fuck, Gray." Jay shook his head. "I don't make the rules. I just follow orders. Now, are you with me? Or do I have to do this myself?" Jay waited, but when Jazzman said nothing, he simply sighed and nodded. "Fine. Wait in the Vee." Jay drew the Gruber pistol and marched towards the humans in the tattered clothes and shot them both point blank in the chest. "Get them in the Humvee," he shouted, waving at the bewildered humans struggling weakly with Sparrow and Marion.

"Boss?"

"I don't want to hear it," Jay said. And then he stopped. "Belay that. Actually, I do want to know. What sex are they?"

"One of each," Sparrow said.

"Good," Jay said. "Get them in the back." He climbed behind the wheel and glanced at Jazzman. "Get on the .50, old man. We still have to get them to the extraction point."

Jazzman nodded and then climbed back behind the machine gun without a word. Jay leaned across the dash to enter the mission status on the screen and was rewarded with a new set of coordinates three kilometres further north.

"Mount up," he shouted as Sparrow and Marion approached the Humvee. "We're leaving." Jay wrinkled his nose as Marion marched the female past the open door. He looked at Scruffette as she perked up on the backseat. "Yeah," he said. "That's what I thought."

19

Beane slung the SUV into the street of Senator Haines' neighbourhood and then stomped his foot on the gas to power the vehicle along the short stretch of road before Haines' house. He bumped it up and over the kerb, through the flowerbeds, before slamming on the brakes outside the front door. The SUV continued its forward motion for a few seconds after Beane leaped from the driver's side, crashing into the porch as Beane rolled to the left, seeking cover against the wall, making sure he ducked beneath the window. He cursed as the first three of Claud's suppressed shots splintered the glass and sent shards cascading down Beane's neck.

If the SUV careening across the senator's lawn, and the splintering of glass didn't wake the neighbours, then Beane's unsuppressed return fire surely would. He might have considered a suppressor if there had been time, but, as he fired two rounds from his Glock G19 at Claud's shadow, he guessed the whole street would soon be awake, and that law enforcement would be on the way shortly after that.

"Worry about that later, Beane," he told himself as he moved along the wall towards the door. He stopped, took a breath, jerked his head around the wall and back again for a quick peek, and then cursed when he saw Bill Haines' body at the bottom of the stairs. "How are you doing, Bill?" he shouted, figuring that Claud knew his position, anyway. "Are you okay?"

Beane cursed again when Bill didn't respond. He rolled his shoulder to his right, in an effort to see if the bathroom light was on, but the eaves of the house restricted his view. Beane ducked back against the wall and looked at the smoked windows of the SUV instead and nodded when he saw a light from the first floor reflecting on the glass on the rear passenger door.

"Okay," he said. "Time to move."

While Rhodium enjoyed listing the qualifications and experience of their team, not all the skills of their employees were listed on the company website. There was even a section inviting interested parties to contact Rhodium for what the company called *Special Services*. Beane was rapidly working his way up through Rhodium's private security section, but while he had worked with Claud in the past, Claudia Baur's history in the company was restricted to the chiefs of the Special Services only. They assured Beane she was both capable and most certainly qualified to join Senator Haines' protection detail. They simply omitted what qualifications she might have.

"Assassin, maybe," Beane whispered as he slid up the wall into a standing position, and then thrust his arms and the pistol in a two-handed grip ahead of him as he took a step around the wall and another into the house.

Other than the splintered door, Bill's body, and the blood trail he left as he slid or crawled down the stairs, there was little damage. What was it Haines had said? She had a nightmare? If that was the case, and it woke her up, then dreaming about the Utahraptor might just have saved the senator's life.

Beane checked his immediate surroundings before crouching beside Bill and checking for a pulse in the side of the man's neck. He kept the Glock trained in front of him, moving it in line with his eyes as he scanned what he could see of the kitchen on his right, and the entrance to the living area on his left. Beane sighed as he felt Bill's weak pulse beneath his fingers, and then, turning his head slightly at the sound of the emergency sirens in the distance, Beane stood up.

"Claud?" he said. "We can talk about this."

Beane took a step towards the kitchen. He glanced into the living area and took a second to consider the most likely position Claud had taken to shoot at him while he ducked beneath the window. He paused as the sound of emergency sirens drew closer.

"Claud?" It was possible, of course, that she had run, choosing to leave before the police arrived. "I would have," Beane whispered as he cleared the kitchen, then moved swiftly through the living area to clear the office space and then through the adjoining door to the garage. He took his time, using as much cover as possible, moving confidently between the gaps with his pistol covering the positions Claud might be when anticipating the route he took through each room.

The sirens grew louder. Beane guessed they were a few minutes away. Claud, he guessed, had run. He moved back through the house, checking Bill's pulse once more on his way up the stairs. He took each step slowly, pistol raised, eyes synced to the iron sight at the end of the pistol as he moved to the first floor. He paused at the top, took a breath, remembered that Haines had a pistol, and cleared his throat just before he reached the bathroom door.

"Senator? It's Beane. The police are on the way."

"Beane?"

"Yes. It's me, Warren. Are you okay?"

"We're okay."

"Tessa's with you?"

"She's here."

"Okay. Stay put while I clear the first floor."

Beane moved past the bathroom, ignoring Haines' concerns about Bill. That could wait. He had to make sure Claud had left the house, that she wasn't simply waiting for Haines' to open the door and then finish the job. Beane moved through each room, Bill's office, Tessa's bedroom, the Haines' bedroom, and the walk-in closet. He paused in each room, forcing himself to listen, to ignore the sirens, to really *listen* for any sound of Claud while he visually searched the rooms for any signs that someone might be hiding in there.

"Nothing," he whispered.

Beane allowed himself to relax, just a tiny bit, and then moved back to the bathroom door.

"Senator?"

"Yes?"

"Unlock the door."

Beane listened as Haines moved inside the bathroom. He took a step back to cover any sudden attack from Claud – most likely from the bedrooms – and then gave Haines his best, albeit economical, most reassuring smile.

"You're okay," he said. "I think she's gone."

"You're sure?"

"Pretty sure."

"And Bill?" Haines lowered her voice. She trembled as she spoke. "You never answered me."

"Bill's hurt. But the paramedics are on their way." Beane nodded as Haines took a breath. "Senator," he said. "It's going to be crazy when the police arrive. I need you to listen to what I tell you now, because if anything happens to me, you're going to have to act alone. Do you understand?"

"What's going to happen to you?" Haines shook her head. "No. No. No. You're my protection. Adler said he would protect me."

"Adler's gone off the rails, Senator," Beane said. "*Reviver* is active. They just blasted a chunk of desert in Libya."

"They're going to fill the desert with dinosaurs?" Haines' eyes narrowed. "It makes no sense. They don't even live long enough to…"

"It's bigger than that." Beane paused at the sound of tyres crunching against the kerb in the street, and the sound of car doors opening. The swirl of red and blue emergency lights flashed into the bathroom. The sirens faded and stopped as the police turned them off. Beane looked at Haines and said, "I talked with the Rhodium team leader in Libya. Adler gave him specific instructions. The dinosaurs and whatever additional life is revived in the desert is secondary. They're looking for something specific."

"What?"

"Us," Beane said. "Or, rather, us… *Homo Ergaster*, actually, if I've got this right."

"What are you talking about?"

"Humans, Senator. The first humans, *Homo Sapiens*. The whole *Reviver Project* is about bringing us back to life in our purest form. He's tasked the Rhodium team with picking up specimens and extracting them from the desert."

"But if they're like the dinosaurs, they'll just die."

Beane shook his head. "Not necessarily. Adler changed the concentration of the ceti particles," he said. "And unlike the dinosaurs, if they get to them in time, it's possible they can keep them alive."

"But what the hell for?"

"You'd have to ask Adler. In fact, you have to ask him publicly."

"No…"

"You have to call a press conference, Senator. Get this out in the open. Without you, there is no oversight. Adler and WARDEV can just blast areas at will, as they go fishing for other specimens."

"More humans?" Haines took a breath, twisting her head as the police approached the door, shouting challenges. "I don't understand it."

"Neither do I, and neither will the people, but if you don't tell them, if you don't challenge him, Adler and his team will continue their fishing expedition, until they've assembled everything they need for whatever purpose they have in mind."

"That's pretty vague, Beane."

Beane's face lit up with the briefest of smiles. "I know. But think about it. The implications are limitless. He's fucking with life itself, and if he can patent that, legally, he's going to change society as we know it. A few short-lived dinosaurs are the smokescreen he needs to pluck what he wants out of the desert. This is…" Beane paused at the sound of the police entering the house, calling for a paramedic. "This is the equivalent of discovering life in outer space. *Reviver* is like a time machine, only he's bringing the past into the future, and the *future* of our species is under threat."

"Beane…"

"I have to go now," he said. "Stay safe. Get police protection, Treasury – not private." Beane called down to the police at the bottom of the stairs. "My name is Jim Beane. I'm with Rhodium Security. I'm contracted to protect Senator Haines. I'm armed. I'm putting down my weapon."

"Show us your hands."

Beane turned to Haines and said, "I'm going now. Good luck." He took a breath and a small step towards the stairs. "I'm putting my gun down," he said, raising his voice. "I'm going to slide it onto the top step." Beane's Glock clattered onto the stairs as he pushed it with the toe of his boot. "I'm coming around the corner," he said. "Don't shoot."

Beane nodded at Haines, and then waved at Tessa as she peeped over the lip of the bathtub. "Your dad's going to be just fine," he said. "The paramedics will take care of him." He nodded at Haines and then stepped around the corner, starting his slow descent of the staircase.

"Gun! He's got a gun!"

Beane barely registered the warning shout, recognising the woman's voice a split second before the first bullet hit him in the chest. The impact pushed him against the wall, knocking the last breath out of his body as he gasped for more. Beane's pistol clattered another two steps, and he reached for it.

It was instinct.

Something he was trained to do, to use his last ounce of energy on a final effort to defend himself and those under his protection.

Haines screamed as the police fired a third shot that punched into Beane's shoulder. Beane tumbled down the stairs, adding more blood to Bill's already staining the wooden steps. The thought that they would never get it out of the grain entered Beane's head in one of those surrealistic moments before the end. But even as the life ebbed out of him, Beane was conscious enough to recognise Claud's face as she stepped around the police officers who had shot Beane, to whisper in his ear.

"*Special Services*, motherfucker," she said.

Beane listened as Claud briefed the police, explaining the nature of the trauma Beane had inflicted on the Haines family, that the senator was confused, maybe even drugged. She was good. He underestimated her, just as he had underestimated Adler and the goals of the *Reviver Project*.

"Senator Haines? This is Claudia Baur, with Rhodium Security. I know you're in shock. I know you're scared, but we've neutralised the threat. The police are coming up the stairs now. They're going to protect you and your family, Senator. Everything is going to be okay."

Claud stepped to one side to give the police room, and then, as they continued up the stairs, she switched Beane's Glock for an identical pistol, casually removing the suppressor with gloved hands before pressing the gun into Beane's palm for the all-important prints.

"Shooting the Senator's husband was unnecessary, Beane," she said, just loud enough for Beane to hear, as she placed her Glock on the stairs at his feet. "Too bad he won't live." Claud leaned in closer to add, "None of them will."

Claud kissed Beane lightly on the cheek and then stepped away. She watched him for a second. And then, as his last breath seeped out of his lungs, she turned and walked away.

20

Fahd struggled with the Toyota as they hit a patch of soft sand. He shifted gears, engaged the four-wheel drive, and then concentrated on driving efficiently without impulsive snatches at the gas pedal for bursts of speed that might get them further bogged down in the dunes. Luci knelt on the passenger seat with her gaze fixed on the Tyrannosaurus Rex stumbling behind them.

"It's still coming, Fahd," she said.

"I know."

"Maybe one hundred feet… Closing."

"Luci."

"It doesn't look well," she said. "It's not steady on its feet. Maybe it's sick. Or maybe the whole process – whatever it was… Maybe it doesn't last?"

"Luci," Fahd said, raising his voice. "There's a camp ahead. Do you see it?"

Luci twisted in her seat and looked through the dusty windscreen at a collection of tents inside a low wall of sand packed into squares of sturdy mesh placed in a perimeter around the camp. There was a small opening in the wall with a gate that hung loosely on its hinges.

"We could shelter inside, maybe?" Fahd said. "There might be radios. We could call for help."

Luci nodded. "Good plan," she said, just as something hard hit the rear of the vehicle, throwing her against the dashboard. Luci hit her head and slumped to the floor and then rolled onto the ceiling of the cab as the forty-foot-long dinosaur batted the HiLux onto its roof.

"Luci!"

Fahd reached for her, but the T-Rex' second attack propelled him out of the vehicle. Luci rolled onto her side as the dinosaur huffed and snorted, prowling around the crumpled vehicle as it tried to press its maw through the windows. Safety glass tumbled into the cab as the T-Rex smashed the windows. Luci lifted her head, tasted blood in her mouth, and then opened her eyes. She froze when she saw the T-Rex' legs less than three feet from her face.

"Oh shit," she whispered.

"Hey!"

Luci turned her head as Fahd shouted at the dinosaur. She saw him wave his arms, saw him jump. And then, when he shouted again, she understood what he was trying to do.

"No," she said. "No. Fahd. Don't."

Fahd caught her eye, and flashed Luci an impossibly brave, but still gorgeously crooked, smile. He dipped his head and pressed his hands together, and, with little more than a nod, he resumed his shouting and waving until the Tyrannosaurus understood that Fahd was the real prize, not the young woman inside the car. The dinosaur lunged after Fahd just as the Libyan ran away from the camp, and away from the car.

Luci scrambled out of the upturned vehicle, shouting Fahd's name, only to see him disappear into the distance. She cursed the ground he walked upon, palming tears from her eyes, sniffing once, wiping her nose with the back of her hand, scratching grit and dust into her skin, just as Sugar's words of encouragement popped into her head, reminding her that Fahd would protect her, that he would probably give his life to do so.

"Well, he just did," Luci said, raising her voice. "He just gave his life for me. And now a dinosaur is going to…" Luci snorted, shaking her head as she listened to herself, catching the words, dissecting them, laughing at them, as nothing she said could possibly be true. "Because they're dead."

She felt the tremor in the sand beneath her feet at the same time as she caught the leathery smell in the air, twisted with something rotten, like old meat – hot and putrid. Luci turned as a second T-Rex staggered towards her. She squinted at it, suddenly curious that it was slightly smaller than the first one, slighter – a juvenile, perhaps.

"Or female?"

Luci held her breath as the dinosaur paused to sniff the air, and then staggering forward, it tripped and slumped to the ground. The earth shook as if a tree had fallen at Luci's feet. She heard the snap of bones in the dinosaur's body, the huff and snort of laboured breathing, and caught each fetid breath in her face as the dinosaur exhaled. Luci looked over her shoulder at the camp, turned towards it, and then paused mid-step.

Luci stopped.

She turned back to the T-Rex and took a small step towards it.

"Easy, girl," she said, taking another cautious step. "I won't hurt you." Luci almost laughed as she realised, "I *can't* hurt you. Even if I could, you don't exist."

And yet, there it was, a female Tyrannosaurus Rex, over sixty million years old, and a couple of continents south of where they had been found. It was breathing – just – and it was whole, with skin, teeth, and eyes the size of Luci's fists, growing smaller by the minute. Luci took another step until she was close enough to reach out and touch the T-Rex' massive, blunt nose if she dared.

Luci exhaled, glancing once more over her shoulder, wondering if Fahd was around, if he was doubling back, or if he was…

"No," she whispered. "Not dead. He's not dead." Luci looked into the T-Rex' eyes. "But you might be dying." She reached out and pressed her palm onto the T-Rex nose, felt the smooth scales on her skin, the sheen of something like oil – sticky, almost dry. And then, with another laboured exhale – softer now – the dinosaur blinked slowly, its eyes closing as Luci worked her way along the length of its snout until she could see her reflection in the Tyrannosaur's eyes. "Hi," she said. She bit her lip, eyes widening as she *connected* with the prehistoric beast. "The one that doesn't exist."

Luci thought of her sister, wondering how she could ever tell her what she had seen. But any further thoughts evaporated in the heat as the dinosaur closed its eyes, and with one last, long exhale, the brief life it had been given departed.

"I don't know what this is about," Luci said. "But I'm going to find out." She swallowed and then looked at the camp once more. She turned back to the dinosaur and then, with one last touch, she walked away, striding to the camp with increasing purpose.

It had to belong to the military, the ones that expelled Sugar and her team from the desert. "And Mazin before that," she said as she reached the gate of the compound. Luci stepped inside.

Crates of equipment were stacked under awnings, with what looked like tinned food and plastic jerry cans of water on the left, flanked by weapons of all descriptions. On the right were more jerry cans, lined up on the sand next to a small vehicle – a two-seater with a bubble canopy, small, balloon-like wheels, and weapons sticking off the sides. Luci nodded as she guessed the buggy was fast.

"I can use it to find Fahd," she said as she took a step closer.

Luci stopped halfway and looked at the gear, food, and water on her left. She nodded and turned in that direction, starting with water – drinking some, stockpiling more. Luci found a vest with pockets for magazines for the weapons in the racks. While she knew next to nothing about guns, she guessed it was more about practice than knowledge, deciding that if Joci could figure it out…

"Then so can I."

She caught herself reaching for a short carbine and shook her head as she tried to put words to what she was thinking, what she was *feeling*. It wasn't just the dead dinosaur, or the fact that it shouldn't be there. It went deeper than that. Yes, she recognised the need to find Fahd. To find him and protect him. But again, *deeper*, there was something about this place – the desert, as if the magic of the sands – bringing all these ancient, prehistoric creatures and vegetation back to life – had led her to this place, to give her the means to protect it.

She laughed.

"Luci Hampton," she said. "Protector of the desert."

Another laugh and then Luci grabbed the carbine, and one more for Fahd. She took two of everything, stuffing the vests and more ammunition behind the seats of the buggy, while strapping extra fuel cans to the sides. She found a map – conveniently – in a canvas case with a plastic window, and the positions of more camps marked in red. She tugged a greasy red crayon from the case and drew a rough ring around the camp, identifying her first search area in which she hoped to find Fahd.

"And more dinosaurs," she said, frowning as she wondered what she was going to do about them.

It struck her then that she was trapped inside a controlled area, patrolled, and guarded, most likely, by the same military…

"Probably a private military contractor," she said, thinking of an article she had once read in connection with security options for field trips in dangerous parts of the world.

… who had visited Sugar and her team.

Luci finished loading the vehicle and then opened the gates. She stuffed a granola bar into her mouth, washed it down with a bottle of tepid water, and then climbed into the buggy. She plucked at a strip of cloth tape stuck to the centre of the steering wheel and read the label.

"*Dodgem Four*. Huh." Luci snorted again. "The Four Horseman of the Apocalypse." She made a show of looking around, adding, "Where are the other three when I need them?"

Luci looked for the keys to start the engine and then found a button she hoped was the ignition, as the thought of firing a salvo of rockets at the weapons racks on the opposite side of the small camp did not inspire the young archaeologist with confidence.

The engine started with an electrical whine, followed by a throaty roar of the petrol engine. Luci grinned as she realised the buggy was roughly the same size as her parents' Mini.

"If a little wider," she said, as she tickled the gas pedal, and then accelerated out of the camp.

Luci whooped as she discovered the buggy was far more responsive, and then hit the brakes, coming to a sudden stop inside a cloud of dust. The dust settled, falling to the ground, adding another layer of grit to her hair, clothes, and skin. And, as the cloud dissipated, Luci saw the inert body of the female Rex.

"You can't exist," she said, staring at it. "But as long as you don't exist, I'll do whatever I can to protect you and your kind." Luci gave a solemn nod, as if she had just vowed to do something, and would stand by what she said. "But first…" Luci clipped the map to the dashboard. "I'll find Fahd."

Luci took one last look at the T-Rex, and then spun the little buggy around the camp as she followed the male Rex' tracks. There was a chance Fahd might have found a rock to crawl under, hiding just long enough to stay alive until the T-Rex ran out of steam.

"Or life," Luci said, as she recalled what had happened to the female.

She wondered again about how it could all come to be. How dinosaurs could roam the earth once more, and what it would take to make that happen? Luci's PhD had focused on filling the gaps in fossil clades with the help of new technology and associated theories – both adapted and untested. But her head began to hurt in the first few seconds she spent wondering what technology was required, and how it would be delivered, to revive dead cells, especially those that had been dead for tens, sometimes hundreds, of millions of years.

She decided not to worry about it.

Which was when she heard the familiar beat of helicopter blades.

Luci slowed to a stop and got out of the vehicle. She shaded her eyes from the sun as she squinted at what looked like a very big helicopter, or perhaps a hybrid sort that was actually a modest-sized plane.

"There," she whispered when she saw it.

Luci watched as more helicopters appeared on the horizon. And then she gasped as she caught the sounds of rapid machine gun fire on the wind and realised she knew what the pilots and gunners were doing.

"No," she breathed, pressing her hand to her mouth. "No…"

21

The team was silent as Jay drove. Sparrow turned his head at each muffled cry from the cargo area of the Humvee, but said nothing, looking away when Jay caught his eye. Scruffette whimpered in the back with Marion, but apart from an unenthusiastic cry of *contact right* and *multiple contacts* from Jazzman in the gunner's position, no one said anything at all.

"Fuck." Jay slammed the steering wheel and then hit the brakes, bringing the two-tonne military vehicle to an abrupt halt. He killed the engine and turned in his seat. "Team meeting," he said with a slap of Jazzman's leg. Jay looked at each of them in turn, and then said, "Out with it."

"With what, sir?" Marion said.

Jay snorted and said, "So, it's *sir* from now on, is it?"

"After you wasted the two men back there," Marion said, matching Jay's hard stare with one of her own. "Yeah, I think so."

"They were already dead."

"Says you."

"I mean, they died already. Whatever this is…" Jay spun his finger in the air. "It's not natural, and it's not on me. So you can park whatever morality trip you're on somewhere else.

We've got a job to do, and believe me..." Jay pointed at the rear of the Humvee. "These are perishable goods. We have to get them to the extraction point. We don't have time for *this*," he said, giving them each another pointed look. "So you're either in or you're out, and I mean, *walking*."

"Right," Jazzman said. "A walking lunch, more like."

"You don't like it, old man?"

"I think you're acting cooler than usual, boss," Jazzman said. "This isn't you."

"No?" Jay shrugged. "Well, it sure as shit isn't the *world* I knew. Something changed in the night, and I guess I did too. Maybe when the natural way of things gets shredded, and everything you thought you knew is no longer what it used to be. Then, hey, maybe I've changed. Maybe we all have."

"Or," Jazzman said, his voice quiet and level. "Maybe you need to tell the team that your mother's real sick..."

"Don't..."

"And she's not coming back when she's gone. Unless, all of this..." Jazzman nodded at the sound of muffled cries and the occasional thump from the rear. "Maybe this is messing with your head, just as much as the dinosaurs."

"Gray..."

"So," Jazzman said. "Here's what we're going to do. We're going to get these..." He paused. "These *people* to the extraction sight. They are cargo. We will deliver. And then we will bug out and get back to base. Then, if anyone's still feeling twitchy about the mission, they can take a good, long look at their termination clauses, and get the fuck out of the desert if they want to. But until then, we need to rally around the boss and get the job done. Agreed?"

"Sure," Sparrow said, without hesitation.

Jazzman turned to look at Marion. "Maid?"

"Just get us home, boss," she said.

"Okay." Jay nodded at Jazzman and then started the engine. "How are we doing?"

"Multiple contacts all around, boss," Jazzman said from behind the machine gun. "Just go straight. I'll clear a path."

"So confident," Sparrow said with a grin. "I look up to him."

"Sure you do," Marion said.

Sparrow laughed and made a show of tilting his head. "No, really. I look *up* to him." He pointed, grinning again until Marion shot him a dirty look and Jay pumped the gas.

"How far?" Jay asked.

"Er, let me see real quick," Sparrow said as he turned to study the screen mounted on the dash. "Yeah, we're close. Less than half a mile. If they're coming by chopper, according to their ETA, they should be there any minute. Hey," Sparrow said, calling up to Jazzman. "See any choppers?"

"Wait one…"

Jay turned his head a little as the sound of an approaching helicopter cut through the roar of the Humvee's engine.

"Yeah, I got one," Jazzman said. "That's three. One tiltrotor and two support. Gunships, I guess."

"See, if we had had a chopper," Sparrow said. "This whole adventure would have been over in minutes."

"Adler didn't want you to have a chopper," Jay said. "He didn't want you to frighten them."

"Who? The people?" Sparrow laughed. "Jay, we're taking them to a chopper. You don't think that's gonna frighten them?"

"What?" Marion said. "More than the two of us grabbing them in the desert and stuffing them in the back of a truck? More than that, Sparrow?"

"Hey," he said, pointing at Jay. "He said Adler didn't want them spooked."

"I'm guessing," Jay said, "he didn't want them spooked before they could save them. The tiltrotor's a big bird. It's probably stuffed with medical supplies. Maybe even a cryochamber."

"A what?"

"Never mind," Jay said. "Just something I saw on TV."

"Well, you don't see *that* on TV," Marion said as she leaned forward. "What the hell is that? An oasis?"

"Check the map," Jay said, clicking his fingers at the screen. "Switch to photo view."

"Yeah, it's green," Sparrow said. "There's water."

"It's like the Serengeti," Marion said. "Now that I did see on TV. It's a watering hole. 'Cept this one is full of dinosaurs."

"Yep." Jay leaned forward as the V-22 Osprey slowed to a hover for landing. He read the company name stencilled on the side and said, "Anyone ever heard of *ShanuTek*?"

"Nope," Sparrow said. "But then yesterday I thought dinosaurs were extinct. So..."

"Funny," Jay said. He pointed at the gunships as they settled into an overlapping orbit at different heights above the tiltrotor. "Let's make this efficient, okay?"

"Sure, boss," Marion said.

"I'll drive right up. You guys get ready with the cargo..." He paused to look at Marion. "The *people*. Jazzman will cover us."

"Got it," Sparrow said.

Jay slowed as they approached the rear of the tiltrotor, resisting the temptation to try to squeeze the Humvee inside, knowing that it was too wide for the cargo area, but that smaller vehicles could be accommodated. He stopped within twenty feet of the ramp. The pilot had shut down the engines and he guessed, despite the risk, it was to reduce the amount of dust and sand blowing around the aircraft.

"Okay, go," Jay said, with a nod for Sparrow and Marion to retrieve their cargo. He stepped out of the Humvee to greet a short, fair-skinned woman with long brown hair tied in a generous bun on top of her head. She wore desert fatigues but gave Jay the impression she was more comfortable wearing a lab coat.

"I'm Dr Hope Teller," she said with a firm shake of Jay's hand. "What have you got for me?"

"Two people – male and female."

"Yes?"

"Found them a few miles back that way." Jay shrugged. "Nothing much to say. We followed your DNA flare. Found them. Picked them up."

"Any trouble?"

"With them?" Jay shook his head.

"And the dinosaurs?"

"Yeah… A bit more trouble."

"Wild though, isn't it?" Teller said with a smile.

"Pretty wild," Jay said.

"Contact," Jazzman said. "Getting closer."

Jay turned to look in the direction Jazzman was pointing, and then squinted at what looked like a small pack of dinosaurs heading their way.

"Ah, Doc," he said. "Any idea what they are?"

He turned around, but Teller was already halfway up the ramp with the cargo, supervising the medical team who took the revived humans out of Sparrow and Marion's hands.

"They're fast, boss," Jazzman said.

"Yeah, I can see that." Jay drew his sidearm and then shouted for Sparrow and Marion to hurry. He raised his voice as the Osprey's engines whined into life and the rotors started to turn. "Okay then," Jay said. "So much for thank you and goodbye."

"What have we got, boss?" Sparrow said as he and Marion jogged the last few feet to the Humvee.

"You're the dinosaur expert," Jay said. "You

tell me."

"Yeah…" Sparrow cupped his hands around his eyes as the tiltrotor stirred up a thick cloud of dust. "No idea. And now I can't see them. I think they might have been…"

Sparrow's last words died on his lips as five-foot of muscle, teeth, and leathery skin burst through the dust cloud and stuck its claws through Sparrow's vest to pierce his chest.

"Fuck…" Jay drew his pistol and spun around. He slammed the muzzle into the tiny dinosaur and blew a hole in its chest with a rapid burst of .50 bullets from the Gruber. Jay emptied the magazine and then kicked the shredded raptor off Sparrow's chest and dragged his bloody comrade to the Humvee. "Jazz! Wounded!"

The dust blew around the Humvee as the Osprey lifted off the sand. Marion appeared in front of Jay. She slapped her Gruber into his hand, shouting something about it being loaded, while she took Jay's weapon, and pulled Sparrow to the rear of the Humvee. Jazzman dropped onto the ground beside Jay. He tugged his carbine into his shoulder.

"Can't use the .50," he said, pointing at the Osprey. "Not 'til they're gone."

"Sparrow's down," Jay shouted. "Some little fucker…"

Jazzman pushed in front of Jay and fired a prolonged burst at a brown shape blundering through the dust cloud. It spun away, and he followed, just a few feet, but deep enough inside the dust cloud that Jay couldn't see him.

"Jazzman!" Jay took a step forward. "Gray?"

Jay spun as something thumped onto the hood of the Humvee. He turned the Gruber on it and let fly with a short burst. The raptor tumbled off the hood and out of sight.

"Jay," Marion yelled from inside the cab. "Grab Scruffette!"

The chocolate Labrador shot out of the Humvee, and into the dust cloud before Jay could catch her. Jay followed a few steps and then stopped. Jazzman was out there with a carbine and Jay didn't fancy getting mistaken for something prehistoric. He returned to the Humvee and looked inside, shaking his head when Marion asked about her dog.

"I'm sorry," he said, holding her gaze for a second before asking about Sparrow.

Marion shook her head. "He bled out faster than I've ever seen."

"Shit." Jay closed his eyes for a second and then closed the door. "Jazzman?"

"Here," he said, as he stumbled towards the Humvee. The dust cloud settled as the Osprey flew away with an escort, leaving one gunship loitering on station, picking targets and scattering dinosaurs as it strafed the oasis with twenty-millimetre rounds.

"Phase Three," Jay said as the gunship set up for a second run. He looked at the blood on Jazzman's vest and said, "Are you hurt?"

"A scratch," Jazzman said. "Deeper than I expected. And I guess no antibiotic we know is gonna kill whatever bug those bastards are carrying." He grinned. "You said the health benefits were good, right?"

"Yeah," Jay said. He nodded at the Humvee. "Sparrow's gone."

"What?"

"And Scruffette took off."

"Dead?"

Jay shrugged. "Not yet," he said, keeping his voice to a whisper. "But we should get back, get some help."

"What about them?" Jazzman said, wincing as he raised a bloody arm to point at a small vehicle charging towards the oasis.

"Is that a dodgem?"

"It sure looks like one," Jazzman said. "I guess they came back."

"Well, I'm not complaining. Although…" Jay paused. "What are they chasing?"

Jay stopped talking as the dodgem slowed to a stop and then let fly with a string of four rockets, all aimed at the sky.

"I don't believe it." Jay glanced at Jazzman a second before the Hellfire rockets slammed into the helicopter gunship, knocking it out of the sky in a sudden ball of flame and thick, oily smoke. The gunship crashed to the left of the oasis with a secondary explosion that sent another black pall of smoke into the sky.

Jazzman looked at Jay and said, "Who?"

"I don't know," Jay said. "But we're not sticking around to find out." He helped Jazzman into the passenger seat, apologised to Marion about leaving the dog behind, and then jogged around the vehicle to climb behind the steering wheel. "New mission," he said. "We go home. Right now." He pointed at the gunner's position. "Marion, you've got the .50."

"On it," she said, after a quick glance out of the window. "Scruffette's smart," she said. "She'll be all right."

Jay caught the look on Marion's face, knew she was lying, but nodded anyway. "Yes," he said. "She will."

Marion nodded and then climbed into the gunner's position. Jay started the engine.

"Hang in there, old friend," he said. "I'm going to get you home." Jay looked at Sparrow's body in the rear and dipped his head in respect. "I'm going to get all of you home."

"And what about them?" Jazzman asked, pointing at the dodgem.

"Fuck them," Jay said. "And fuck Adler and whatever side mission he's given whoever they are. We're going home."

Marion thumped the roof. "Contact right," she shouted before opening up with the machine gun. Jay spun the wheel and stomped his foot on the gas, gritting his teeth as the Humvee lurched forward. "Contact," Marion shouted again, turning the machine gun on the mount and pumping more rounds into the targets to their left.

Thud. Thud. Thud. Thud.

"Contact right."

Thud. Thud. Thud.

"Multiple contacts…"

22

Glenn Adler checked his look in the mirror when the makeup artist had finished dusting his cheeks with a little powder to reduce the glare from the stage lights. The barber had done a good job on Adler's beard, and the touch of dark grey he had added to some of the lighter strands in Adler's hair, they said, made him look at least ten years younger.

Either that, or they're far too polite.

Adler didn't care.

This was *his* day. The day when he came out of the shadows, and took his place in history, as the man behind the *Reviver Project*, the greatest breakthrough in medicine since the discovery of penicillin.

"Alexander Fleming," Adler whispered as he stood up. "March 7, 1929." He thanked the makeup artist, gave the barber a warm handshake and then waved to his assistant that he was ready.

"Here's the latest and *last* draft of your speech," she said, with emphasis, pressing a series of small cards into Adler's hands. "The teleprompter is ready. Please remember to look at it."

"Gillian," Adler said. "Stop fussing."

"I will fuss, Mr Adler. That's what ShanuTek

pays me to do." Gillian dipped her head to look over her thick-rimmed glasses. "I'm very good at it."

"I noticed."

"Just two more things," Gillian said, as Adler took a step towards the door.

"Yes?"

"We'll be patching Dr Teller in through a live, but, honestly, very shaky connection. She is flying, after all."

"And Dr Green?"

"Yes," Gillian said. "Dr Green."

"You'll patch him through, too?"

"On an unfortunately shaky connection," Gillian said. "It's not certain we can stream him into the conference. But we have a nice graphic to use as a placeholder." She paused, adding, "I think it's for the best. Don't you?"

"Yes," Adler said. "And the second thing?"

"There's a woman to see you. She's waiting in the SCIF."

"Thank you, Gillian." Adler tucked the cue cards into his jacket pocket. "I'll see you on stage."

"You have fifteen minutes, Mr Adler."

Adler nodded and then followed Gillian out of the dressing room, turning right when she pointed him in the direction of the portable SCIF ShanuTek had arranged to be delivered to California State University. More of a phone box than a *facility*, Adler wondered what people would think when he squeezed into it together with the leggy blonde he knew as Claud.

"You found me," he said as he closed the door.

"Not difficult, Mr Adler," Claud said. "You posted your itinerary online."

"Yes, well, Ms Baur. It's time to come out of the shadows."

Claud gestured at the room and smiled. "Is it?"

"Some shadows, at least." Adler switched gears and said, "Where are we?"

"Beane's gone."

"I heard," Adler said. "And the senator?"

"Secure."

"Dead?"

"*Distressed*," Claud said. "She's taking some time to grieve for her dead husband, and the attempt her previous head of security made on her life."

"Beane?"

"The same."

"And the daughter?"

"Never saw me," Claud said. "And Haines is in a secure ward, on some serious antidepressants. The girl is with her grandparents." Claud shrugged. "Nothing to worry about."

"You're sure?"

"I can remove her if you want?"

"No," Adler said. "Keep her in play. We might need her later once the senator has been weaned off her drugs."

"And the Rhodium team in the desert?"

"Rhodium will deal with that. I understand one of the team is dead, another is comatose with strange bacteria that seems to confound all the doctors he has seen."

"Leaving two alive."

"Alive and well compensated. We might need them at a later date, too. Although…" Adler frowned.

"Yes?"

"The woman, Maid Marion, I think they call her." Adler looked up. "I think she could be used as leverage. It will be easier to control the Warbird if we isolate him."

"When?"

"At your discretion," Adler said, adding, "But make it messy."

"Messy is what I do best," Claud said.

"Yes," Adler said, choosing not to ask. "I'll transfer sufficient funds to your accounts, as agreed."

"Perfect," Claud said.

Adler nodded once and moved towards the door, stopping when Claud stepped in front of him.

"Is there something else, Ms Baur?"

"WARDEV."

"Yes?"

"Another smokescreen?"

"Partly," Adler said. "They had their uses. They green-lit a lot of projects, and got *Reviver* through a lot of hoops and, ultimately, into orbit. But they miscalculated."

"How so?"

"There's no future in warfare, Ms Baur." Adler tapped the notes in his pocket and said,

"The future is, and always has been, in medicine. Humans can kill each other as often and as many times as they like. But if they want to come back and have another go, it will cost them dearly. That," Adler said, with a smile, "is the future."

"And before that?"

"Geriatrics," Adler said with a wink. He nodded at the door, and Claud stepped to one side to let him leave.

"Geriatric Medicine is the new gold rush in medicine. We are living longer than ever before." Adler said. He shuffled his cards on the podium in front of him, ignoring the teleprompter and the scowl pasted on Gillian's face. "Studies show that the US alone needs a minimum of 20,000 new geriatrics doctors to meet the growing demands of the older population. And that's just in the United States. Worldwide? At a guess, to meet the demands of healthy Europeans alone, you would need ten times the number of doctors. In Europe. Now…" Adler walked to the front of the stage and gestured at the students, faculty, and guests seated in front of him. "War and pandemics take their toll. Of course they do. But what if I told you that we at ShanuTek can solve all geriatric problems? All of them." He took a beat to let it sink in. "Today, I'm going to tell you how."

Adler paused for applause, dipping his head in mock humility before lifting his chin and looking out at the audience.

"Thank you," he said as they settled. "Thank you."

"We love you, Mr Adler!"

The audience murmured and tittered as Adler smiled and waved at the heckler.

"And thank *you*," he said, pointing vaguely into the seats at the very back of the auditorium. When they settled and the room was quiet again, Adler nodded. He took a shallow breath and said, "My name is Glenn Adler, and it's my pleasure to present to you today the greatest breakthrough in medicine since the discovery of penicillin."

The audience erupted into thunderous applause until Jay Styles found the remote and muted the television. He placed the remote quietly on the table beneath the flatscreen television mounted on the wall and crossed the room to look out of the window. Brilliant blue waves crashed upon a golden beach, bathed in the evening light of a gentle sun. He looked at his mother in the bed and crossed the floor to sit in the chair beside her. Jay took his mother's hand and smiled as she tried her best to grip it.

"Not so tight, mom," he said.

"Oh, Jay," she said. "Don't tease me."

"I wouldn't," he said. "You just need to rest. The doctors said the new medicine would take its toll. You won't feel the effects straight away, remember? Mom?"

"I know," she said. "But everything you've done for me… I just don't know how to thank you."

"You don't have to." Jay squeezed his mother's hand. "I always said I'd take care of you. It just took a lot longer than expected. And I'm sorry about that."

"Oh, Jay. It's all right."

Jay held her hand as his mother closed her eyes. She snored once, laughed as it woke her up, and then drifted off to sleep again. It had been less than a week since they dragged him out of the desert. They moved his mother to the ShanuTek hospice before he arrived in the States. Jay shook his head as remembered the paperwork, and how it had taken longer to sign his name on the waivers and disclaimers, than it had to fly home.

He looked up at a knock on the door and nodded when the nurse asked if he had time to speak to the doctor.

"Sure," he said, as he laid his mother's hand gently on the bed. "I'll be right there."

Jay found the doctor in a spacious office together with two lawyers.

"Ah, Mr Styles," the doctor said as he stood up to greet him. "We want to accelerate your mother's treatment, but to do that, we need to run a few things by you. Is that all right?"

"Sure," Jay said.

"And is this a good time?"

Jay nodded.

"Wonderful," the doctor said. He gestured at the table. "I'll call for refreshments. This could take some time."

Jay resisted the urge to say *no shit* and pulled out a chair. He nodded at the lawyers, shook their hands when they introduced themselves, and promptly forgot their names. He doubted he would see them ever again.

"Here we are," the doctor said, as his secretary arrived with a tray of fresh coffee and a selection of pastries. "The coffee is heavenly," he said, with a nod to his secretary. "Where did you say it was from, Marge?"

"Colombia," she said. "When you look into it," she said. "It's like looking into the cosmos."

"Yes," the doctor said. "Exactly." He sat down as soon as Marge left. "Marge likes to think she discovered it, but in truth…" He paused, as if wondering whether he should continue. "In truth, I read about it in the transcripts of a psychiatric patient. She was rambling about Colombian coffee and the beans. She mentioned the beans a lot." The doctor shrugged and gestured at the stack of papers in front of Jay. "How are we doing?"

"We're good," he said, flexing his fingers. "Just warming up."

The doctor and the lawyers laughed. Jay put on his best smile, but as they slid the first papers across the table, pointing out the yellow stickers with the arrow guiding him to the sections he should sign, Jay's mind drifted to the desert.

They flew Sparrow's body home on a transport plane, together with Jazzman, sealed up in a plastic bubble with an oxygen mix flowing through it. Gray was Jazzman's name, but it could have been his colour, as his healthy dark brown skin paled and his gaze wandered, unfocused. Marion offered to fly home with him, but

Rhodium put her on a separate flight, flanked by a lawyer who reminded her of her non-disclosure agreements, and wrote up new NDAs on the spot as he thought about them.

Jay flew a day later, following a rigorous Rhodium debrief.

"Tell us again, Jay," they had said. "Who was in the dodgem?"

"I don't know."

"But you ordered them back to base."

"The two in our patrol? Yes."

"And yet a single vehicle returned."

"You know it did," Jay said. "But I don't know from where. You've talked to the guys who came out with us."

"Yes."

"And it wasn't them." Jay shrugged. "You know as much as I do."

"What we know, Mr Styles, is that a small, heavily armed vehicle took out a Rhodium helicopter gunship with a missile." The man paused. "Three missiles."

"Four," Jay said. "Missiles, any idiot can operate."

"Yes…" The man reached for his coffee. "Apparently."

Jay waited for him to continue, but the man simply started again. And on it went, over and over, the same thing, until even the guy from Rhodium had had enough.

After that, everything was turned off.

Zero information.

Just a never-ending pile of papers and small

yellow stickers where Jay should sign away his rights, his mother's rights, and the rights of his children – if he chose to start a family in the future.

Jay paused as he spotted another *future offspring* clause in the latest swathe of legal documents.

"Everything all right, Jay?" the doctor asked.

"Yeah," Jay said.

"But you have a question?"

"Maybe," he said. Jay tapped the paper with the top of the pen. "These future family clauses."

"Yes?"

"I still don't quite understand them."

"Well," the doctor said with a glance at the lawyers. "It's quite simple, really. It's all about DNA. And…" He laughed. "Well. Let's put it this way, Mr Styles. All this…" The doctor made a gesture that encompassed the hospital. "It's expensive. And, simply put, you haven't got the funds, Mr Styles. At least, not in your bank account. But your *body* account is…" He laughed again. "It's loaded, Mr Styles. And I don't think you ever have to worry about running out of capital."

"You mean DNA?"

"Yes, Mr Styles," the doctor said. "Your DNA. Your family's DNA, and whatever the hell we want to do with it." The doctor presented Jay with a straight face, held it for a few seconds, and then burst out laughing. "I'm kidding, Jay. Just kidding. Have some coffee. It's Colombian."

"Just kidding," Jay said, and laughed. But a

glance at the papers in front of him told him it was no joke.

23

After the incident with the helicopter, Fahd made Luci promise she would only ever travel at night. He taught her how to travel in the desert, how to recognise and avoid quicksand, where to find water, and the best places to store the equipment they plundered from the camps before Rhodium emptied them. He tested her on her knowledge of the stars, teasing her when she got them wrong.

"I should have let the T-Rex eat you," Luci said, slapping Fahd's arm as she leaned against his side to trace Draco with the tip of the finger, when she should have been tracing The Big Dipper. She found Fahd trapped in the mouth of a shallow cave with a frustrated Tyrannosaurus Rex thrashing at the rocks in a confused death throe before its body gave out and the big beast collapsed. Fahd liked to say he rescued himself, but they both knew he could never have gotten out of the cave if Luci hadn't found a rope, and pulled him through a hole in the top, as the entrance was blocked by the dead dinosaur.

"I just don't understand how you can know all the dinosaurs and plants from all around the world, but you can't grasp the names of the stars."

"Not my field," Luci said. She slipped her arm through Fahd's and pressed her head against his shoulder, happy to let the black velvet night wrap its gentle fingers around them. She settled for a moment, perhaps less, and then reached for the night vision goggles in Fahd's lap.

He sighed as Luci pressed the goggles to her eyes. "Another one?"

"Write this down," Luci said.

Fahd reached for a pad and clicked on a red penlight.

"Brachiosaurus," Luci said. "Write that down."

"I can't spell it."

"Never mind," Luci said. "Just write BS."

Fahd laughed. "My English is improving, but even I knew what *BS* was before I met you."

"Three of them," Luci said, ignoring him. "It's been eight days since that night in the cave. The T-Rex died within twenty-four hours. But this is bigger, and..." Luci lowered the goggles and bit her lip as she thought. "Unless..."

"Unless *what*?"

"There were herds at the oasis. Before the helicopter came, they were drinking. What if there's something in the water?"

"Or just *water*," Fahd said. "These things, beasts, brought back to life... They would be thirsty." Fahd shrugged. "Simple, eh?"

"Well..." Luci frowned, not quite ready to accept that it could be *that* simple. "Maybe."

"I think so," Fahd said. "And I also think I am tired. I know I am. I'm going to find some food. And then I'm going to bed."

"I'll be down later," Luci said. "I'm just

going to sit for a while."

She reached for Fahd's fingers as he stood up, clutching them for a moment until he pulled away and she let him go. She watched him over her shoulder as he picked his way through the boulders to the cave entrance.

Another cave, Luci thought as she reached for the notepad.

Luci flicked through the pages, running through the butcher's bill of dead dinosaurs they had identified, together with a list of smaller animals, the odd camel, and signs of a distinctively human struggle beneath the sands which Luci wasn't ready to admit to yet.

They had talked about it, about how it made sense for other dead things to be brought back to life. But as they had found so little evidence, Luci guessed that the only dead humans – old or otherwise – to be revived, would be those that had died in a cave.

"And we've been in a lot of caves, and the caves protected us from whatever it was that happened. So…" Luci shrugged as she considered the other option, that humans were simply too weak to break out of the sands on revival, unless the sands beneath which they had died had thinned or shifted.

Zombies wasn't a word Luci used in her scientific vocabulary, but recent evidence suggested she might have to start.

"Not tonight," she said, as she flicked through the pages to the back of the notebook where she kept the list of dinosaurs they had observed that were still living. It was a modest list of less than one hundred living dinosaurs. "Including one more Brachiosaurus," she said, entering the new sighting, date, and time into the notebook.

The list was mostly herbivores, although Fahd was certain he had seen another T-Rex, and fresh prints that belonged to something smaller and faster. The list was a work in progress, and until Luci found a way out of the Rhodium enclosure, she decided she would make it her mission to maintain and add to the list for as long as she could.

"Or until the food runs out."

Luci put the pen down and pulled her battered copy of *The Rubáiyát of Omar Khayyám* out of the pocket at the front of her battle vest. She thumbed through the pages until she came to the passage that suddenly made sense.

"*And those who husbanded the Golden Grain,*" Luci read aloud. "*And those who flung it to the Winds like Rain, Alike to no such aureate Earth are turn'd…*" She paused, tracing her finger beneath the words of the last line. "*As, buried once, Men want dug up again.*"

Fahd had said there was something in the air that night, something in the heavens which might be the *Golden Grain* flung upon the earth.

"The *aureate,*" Luci said. "The *golden* earth."

The last part was easy enough, but the motive was lacking. Understanding what it was all for was the part that made Luci's head ache. She looked to the west, and the section of the perimeter wall Fahd said was closest. The answer lay beyond that wall, and while Luci desperately wanted to discover it, she refused each and every time Fahd suggested they leave.

"My work is here," she said when he pressed her.

"Your work is gone. Sugar is gone. Moved on by the military."

"But Mazin…"

Fahd shook his head each time she tried to use Mazin as a reason to stay. "Mazin? I have seen, with these eyes, the very creatures Dr Mazin found. Only the ones I have seen are not dead. Not yet. Mazin's birds…"

"Ornithischians," Luci said.

"Yes, the word I cannot say. Them. They are alive. They are here. We can go."

"They're trying to kill them, Fahd."

"And the T-Rex has tried to kill me. It tried to kill you. And I think the longer we stay *inside* the wall, the more things we will find that want to eat us. They are living longer," he said. "You said so. The longer they live, the hungrier they get. There is no rain in the desert. The veget…"

"Vegetation."

"Yes. That. It needs water, just like the dinosaurs. It dies."

"Not at the oasis."

"And the soldiers know that, Luci," Fahd said. "It is where they go to kill the dinosaurs." He pointed at her notebook every time they had the same argument. "Your list is getting shorter and shorter. One day there will be nothing left, because the soldiers will have killed everything."

"And on that day," Luci said. "We can go."

"Not before?"

"No."

"And what about your family? Are they not worried?"

"They think I'm in California, Fahd. In the Mojave. They're not worried *yet*."

"But one day…"

"Yes," Luci said. "Probably."

And so the argument went, every time, until Luci said Fahd could leave whenever he wanted to, holding her breath while she waited for his reply, letting it out when he shook his head.

"Not yet," he would say. "But one day…"

One day drifted into the next, as they slept through the heat, adjusting their body clocks to explore at night, taking *Dodgem Four* deeper and deeper into the desert, mapping the boundaries of the first perimeter wall, visiting the camps, plundering, and melting away when they spotted signs of activity. Fahd said he felt like a guerrilla, while Luci dubbed them an anti poaching team, protecting prehistoric beasts from trophy hunters.

They visited the carcasses, too. Documenting decay for the purposes of science, comparing what Luci had read with what she now had seen.

And then, in between the observing, documenting, listing, and plundering, there were flashpoints when they came too close to, or were surprised by, a military patrol. Luci understood she had killed men, maybe even women, when she shot down the helicopter. But she explained it away as a necessary evil, preventing the slaughter of the dinosaurs at the oasis.

It wasn't quite so easy to justify the more personal firefights in the desert.

One in particular kept Luci awake during the day when she should be resting.

When the first glimpses of dawn lit the desert, when Fahd said he was tired, and Luci said she would stay a while longer, she spent the time thinking of the man she killed. She saw his face, his moustache, the freckles beneath his eyes when she stared at him through the scope of the carbine she had taken from the camp. He had caught them unawares. Fahd filled the dodgem with fuel from a jerry can, while Luci relieved herself behind a dune. When she returned, when she saw the man pointing his rifle at Fahd, she sought cover, sliding into position, sighting the carbine on the man, staring at him through the scope.

She spent those pre-dawn moments wondering if it could have turned out differently.

What if she hadn't pulled the trigger?

What if Fahd had simply given himself up?

Would she have done the same?

"No," Luci whispered into the fading night.

She shot him once in the chest. It had been so easy, she almost wondered if she had done it, if she had really killed a man? But the blood that ebbed out of the hole in his body, and the way Fahd shook his head when Luci, suddenly conscious of what she had done, wanted to save him.

"He is dead, Luci," Fahd said. "There is

nothing you can do."

"Nothing?"

Fahd pointed at the man's blood spilling into the sand and shook his head. "Nothing."

"Three," Luci said, looking at the other list she kept on the page with the dog-eared corner folded down to mark it. "The soldier. Two pilots."

Luci closed the notebook and stared at the stars. She searched for The Big Dipper, found something she thought might be *close enough*, and then closed her eyes. The stars became freckles, as she knew they would. And the velvet black sky turned to blood. Perhaps, if she was honest with herself, she would understand that her reluctance to leave had less to do with exposing the truth of what had occurred in the desert, or sharing breakthrough science with the community and making a name for herself, but rather the knowledge that she had changed, that Lucille Hampton of Churlington Hawley could never be the same.

Not ever.

It was, as Jamillah had said, a sickness, for which there was no cure.

Luci was desert sick, doomed to be forever bound to the sands and the velvet night sky above it. She could never leave, and nor did she want to.

"This is my home now," she whispered, opening her eyes to stare into the dawn light. "It's where I belong."

Luci turned her head as Fahd returned. Her nose twitched as she caught the scent of coffee. Luci smiled as Fahd pressed a mug into her hand

and then sat beside her.

"You've been thinking," he said, as they toasted the desert with a soft clink of enamel cups.

"Yes."

"And what have you discovered?" Fahd put his coffee down to light a cigarette.

"That you lie," she said. "Every night you say you are tired. And every single night, you return with coffee."

"Yes," Fahd said. "But you didn't answer me. What have you discovered?"

Luci leaned her head against Fahd's shoulder and sighed.

"I'm sick, Fahd," she said. "I'm sick with the desert."

Fahd dipped his head to look at her and smiled.

"That's good," he said. "It's very good."

Fahd smoked. Luci sipped her coffee, and in the distance, reaching into the dawn, the dinosaurs raised their long trunks and turned their heads to greet the light.

The End

About the Author

Christoffer Petersen is the author's pen name. He lives in Denmark. Chris started writing stories about Greenland while teaching in Qaanaaq, the largest village in the very north of Greenland – the population peaked at 600 during the two years he lived there. Chris spent a total of seven years in Greenland, teaching in remote communities and at the Police Academy in the capital of Nuuk.

Chris continues to be inspired by the vast icy wilderness of the Arctic and his books have a common setting in the region, with a Scandinavian influence. He has also watched enough Bourne movies to no longer be surprised by the plot, but not enough to get bored.

You can find Chris in Denmark or online here:

www.christoffer-petersen.com